KATISH

Ekaterina Pavlovna Beleav. (Katish)

Wanda L. Frolov

Katish

Our Russian Cook

Ruth Reichl

SERIES EDITOR

Illustrated by Henry Stahlhut

Introduction by Marion Cunningham

THE MODERN LIBRARY

NEW YORK

2001 Modern Library Paperback Edition

Series introduction copyright © 2001 by Ruth Reichl
Introduction copyright © 2001 by Marion Cunningham
Copyright © 1947 by Wanda L. Frolov

This edition published by arrangement with Farrar, Straus & Giroux,
LLC. All rights reserved.

LIBRARY OF CONGRESS CATALOGING-IN-PUBLICATION DATA

Frolov, Wanda L.
Katish, our Russian cook / Wanda L. Frolov ; illustrated by Henry
Stahlhut.—Modern Library paperbacks ed.
p.   cm. — (Modern Library food)
ISBN 0-375-75761-9
1. Cookery, Russian. I. Title. II. Series.
TX723.3 .F59   2001
641.5947—dc21   00-068706

Modern Library website address: www.modernlibrary.com

Printed in the United States of America

2   4   6   8   9   7   5   3   1

Introduction to the Modern Library Food Series

Ruth Reichl

My parents thought food was boring. This may explain why I began collecting cookbooks when I was very young. But although rebellion initially inspired my collection, economics and my mother's passion fueled it.

My mother was one of those people who found bargains irresistible. This meant she came screeching to a halt whenever she saw a tag sale, flea market, or secondhand store. While she scoured the tables, ever optimistic about finding a Steuben vase with only a small scratch, an overlooked piece of sterling, or even a lost Vermeer, I went off to inspect the cookbooks. In those days nobody was much interested in old cookbooks and you could get just about anything for a dime.

I bought piles of them and brought them home to pore over wonderful old pictures and read elaborate descriptions of dishes I could only imagine. I spent hours with my cookbooks, liking the taste of the words in my mouth as I lovingly repeated the names of exotic sauces: soubise, Mornay, dugléré. These things were never seen around our house.

As my collection grew, my parents became increasingly baffled.

"Half of those cookbooks you find so compelling," my mother complained, "are absolutely useless. The recipes are so old you couldn't possibly use them."

How could I make her understand? I was not just reading recipes. To me, the books were filled with ghosts. History books left me cold, but I had only to open an old cookbook to find myself standing in some other place or time. "Listen to this," I said, opening an old tome with suggestions for dinner on a hot summer evening. I read the first recipe, an appetizer made of lemon gelatin poured into a banana skin filled with little banana balls. "When opened, the banana looks like a mammoth yellow pea pod," I concluded triumphantly. "Can you imagine a world in which that sounds like a good idea?" I could. I could put myself in the dining room with its fussy papered walls and hot air. I could see the maid carrying in this masterpiece, hear the exclamations of pleasure from the tightly corseted woman of the house.

But the magic didn't work for Mom; to her this particular doorway to history was closed. So I tried again, choosing something more exotic. "Listen to this," I said, and began reading. " 'Wild strawberries were at their peak in the adjacent forests at this particular moment, and we bought baskets of them promiscuously from the picturesque old denizens of the woods who picked them in the early dawn and hawked them from door to door.... The pastry was hot and crisp and the whole thing was permeated with a mysterious perfume.... Accompanied by a cool Vouvray,... these wild strawberry tarts brought an indescribable sense of well-being....' "

"Anything?" I asked. She shook her head.

Once I tried reading a passage from my very favorite old cookbook, a memoir by a famous chef who was raised in a small village in the south of France. In this story he recalls being sent to the butcher when he was a small boy. As I read I was transported to Provence at the end of the nineteenth century. I could see the village with its small stone houses and muddy streets. I could count the loaves of bread lined up at the *boulangerie* and watch the old men hunched over glasses of red wine at the café. I was right there in the kitchen as the boy handed the carefully wrapped morsel of meat to his mother, and I watched her put it into the pot hanging in the big fireplace. It sizzled; it was so real to me that I could actually smell the daube. My mother could not.

But then she was equally baffled by my passion for markets. I could stand for hours in the grocery store watching what people piled into their carts. "I can look through the food," I tried to explain. "Just by paying attention to what people buy you can tell an awful lot about them." I would stand there, pointing out who was having hard times, who was religious, who lived alone. None of this interested my mother very much, but I found it fascinating.

In time, I came to understand that for people who really love it, food is a lens through which to view the world. For us, the way that people cook and eat, how they set their tables, and the utensils that they use all tell a story. If you choose to pay attention, cooking is an important cultural artifact, an expression of time, place, and personality.

I know hundreds of great cookbooks that deserve to be rescued from oblivion, but the ones I have chosen for the Modern Library Food Series are all very special, for they each offer more than recipes. You can certainly cook from these books, but you can also read through the recipes to the lives behind them. These are books for cooks and armchair cooks, for historians, for people who believe that what people eat—and why—is important.

Sirs:

Thank you so much for sending me *Katish*. . . . I've been watching her every move in *Gourmet* and am delighted to see her all-in-one-piece and on my own shelf. I think I've copied every one of the recipes as they've appeared. . . .

It's a delightful book, and perhaps the best thing about it is that the things it talks about can be *made* . . . so often in "literary cookbooks" the recipes are not so good as they sound. My husband in spite of twelve years in Russia was convinced that all mushrooms are poison until he tasted Katish's sour cream dream.

M.F.K. Fisher
Los Angeles, California
December 1947

INTRODUCTION

Marion Cunningham

Wanda Frolov's *Katish* is really two wonderful books smoothly woven into one. The first is about Katish, a young Russian émigré. It takes place during the late 1920s, when Katish, who was widowed during the Russian Revolution and was among the lucky few who escaped to China and Japan and were able to obtain visas for the United States, arrived on the West Coast and settled in Los Angeles.

Her story unfolds as she becomes the cook and housekeeper for a large family. Almost immediately she becomes appreciated for the wonderful food she prepares, and for her cheerful and generous manner. She is also very creative at solving problems; her innocence and desire to help others make her solutions fascinating. And the way she helps other Russian émigrés with what little money she has is nothing short of brilliant. The story of Katish and the members of the eccentric family she worked for and lived with is funny and touching.

The second book is about Russian home cooking at its best. Most of the dishes are simple, created with ordinary ingredients but made to taste wonderful. Katish is as gifted a cook as she is talented at smoothing the way for her loved ones. There are almost eighty recipes, all of which are written in a narrative style containing directions and essential information that only a fine home cook could understand that other cooks would need. There are many additional, intuitively sound, instructions, such as "always salt your ingredients before cooking, as this brings the best flavor forth." Katish's recipes are a gift to all of us home cooks. I've just bought sour cream, plus some other basic ingredients, so I can make some of her fine dishes.

I have been a home cook for almost seventy years, and even today I am still happiest cooking and baking in my own kitchen. Some of the recipes I have made and loved in the past are Russian favorites such as borscht (beet and cabbage soup garnished with sour cream), cabbage rolls stuffed with seasoned ground meat, chicken Kiev, beef Stroganoff, lamb pilaf, cheesecake, and cold zabaglione. These are just a few examples of wonderful classic Russian dishes—the ones closest to Katish's heart—that won over her adoptive family in the New World. Most Russian recipes are inexpensive to make, and they are just as delicious as the most extravagant dishes. Money has nothing to do with taste; it all depends on the talent of the cook. There is an old Russian saying, "Cooks never starve."

With Katish's recipes, not only will you not starve, you will eat the most sublime and comforting food. It was easy to see from this book how the famously sensitive Russian soul was nourished by such a cuisine.

———

From 1972 to 1983, MARION CUNNINGHAM assisted James Beard with his cooking classes across the United States. She is the author of numerous cookbooks, including *The Fannie Farmer Cookbook, The Breakfast Book, The Supper Book,* and, most recently, *Learning to Cook with Marion Cunningham.* A food columnist for the *San Francisco Chronicle* and the *Los Angeles Times,* she lives in California.

KATISH

CHAPTER ONE

My aunt Martha was a woman of firm character and an itching sense of responsibility. Though she was Father's younger sister, she had always felt competent to advise him in matters financial, marital, or moral. Father was used to her and he would nod gravely at her over his pipe and go on with his thoughts, hardly hearing a word she said. But when Father died, Mother was left pretty much at Aunt Martha's mercy, for Mother had always been sorry for this well-intentioned sister-in-law who had never had a husband or children of her own on whom to exercise her passion for management.

Fortunately, a good part of Aunt Martha's improving energies found an outlet in organized charities. Mother felt vastly relieved when she began to take an interest in the Russian émigrés who were arriving on the Pacific Coast in the early twenties. They were some of the refugees from the Russian revolution who had poured into China and Japan and had been among the lucky few to obtain visas for America. But even these charitable interests had a way of back-firing on Mother.

I had just come in from school one afternoon when I saw my aunt's high, old-fashioned electric coupé pull up at our door. She felt that an electric was the only really lady-like mode of transportation still available; she would have preferred a carriage and pair if she could have afforded the outlay and upkeep. Though Aunt Martha must have been hardly forty in 1924, in spirit she belonged to an earlier generation. Her clothes, too, were of another period, for at a time when fashions denied the existence of feminine bosoms and merely hinted at a waistline surprisingly located where it must be sat upon, she presented a well-corseted hourglass figure.

Whenever she visited our white clapboard house in West Los Angeles, her walk up the garden path provided two fine topics for advice. First, there was the extravagantly large garden which Mother insisted upon keeping up, when in the growing city it could have been sold as a building lot; and second, there was the frankly old-fashioned aspect of the house. Aunt Martha insisted that Mother should follow the prevailing mode for putting a plaster false-front on old houses and dubbing them Spanish Colonial. Not to do so was to allow the value of the property to go down. Los Angeles was indulging in an orgy of pale pink, dull orange, and even lavender stucco bungalows that looked more edible than livable. But today, it was easy to see that our relative had more pressing matters to discuss. She nipped up the garden path without so much as a disapproving glance at the bright flower beds.

"I've found just the girl for you, Mary!" she announced breathlessly to Mother the minute she entered the living room.

"Girl? What are you talking about, Martha?"

"Why, a girl to cook for you, and to help with the housework, of course. You know we were discussing the Swedish girl I found last week and you thought she wouldn't be suitable. Now Katish is different—she was made for you."

Katish, Aunt Martha explained, talking very fast so that Mother couldn't interpose any objections, was Ekaterina Pavlovna Belaev; she was a young Russian woman, of good but simple family, widowed in the war. After the revolution, she had made her way with admirable courage and resourcefulness through Russian Turkestan and the wilder outer regions of China to Harbin and then to America. She knew little English, though she had studied diligently during the months that she had waited in Harbin for her American visa.

She had not been trained to earn a living, but she was an excellent cook, and naturally as neat and clean as a new pin. She didn't expect a large salary, but she was in urgent need of a good home, and how could Mother, who claimed to be a Christian, turn her away?

Mother looked uncomfortable. I thought she was weakening. Bub, my fourteen-year-old brother, who had come in by this time, took up the cudgels in defense of the family. "Aw, Mother, we don't want any old foreign cook," he protested. "I like your cooking. Why don't you get this woman a job with some of your rich friends, Aunt Martha?"

Aunt Martha hedged. It was evident that her wealthier friends had been tried and found not wanting an untrained servant. "Well, Mary," Aunt Martha said, nettled into imprudence, "I don't see what you can do but take this poor girl for a time, because I've already promised her that you would."

At this barefaced statement Mother rallied and said quite firmly that she not only did not need a cook; she wasn't going to have one, and her sister-in-law could get out of the matter in the best way she could.

Bub and I rejoiced in Mother's victory. Aunt Martha's protégés were apt to be peculiar—occasionally they were alarming. The last time Mother had succumbed to her appeal to the Christian spirit, we had found ourselves with a cook who took no pains to disguise her triumphant certainty that the whole family was headed for perdition. This worried us for a week, until we found out that the poor woman was a member of one of those queer religious sects which flourished under the warm Southern California sun. She believed that bodily comfort was a sin and she announced her intention of sleeping on a pallet on her bedroom floor. This was all right with Mother, but it was something of a shock to learn that she had gone so far as to sell the bed which Mother had provided— bedstead, springs, and mattress—and contribute the proceeds to her church. Mother discovered this strange evidence of religious zeal on the same day that the cook discovered that we occasionally used liquor in cooking. The cook departed forthwith, adding the vociferous threat of jail for our liquorous iniquities to her previous threats of damnation. The experience had not left us in a receptive mood toward Aunt Martha's suggestions.

Our redoubtable relative seemed to accept Mother's refusal this time. For a week she was sweet and agreeable and appeared to have forgotten all about the needy Russians. But one afternoon Bub and I came in from school to find Katish established in our kitchen!

Mother hurried us upstairs to explain and admonish us to civilized behavior. Aunt Martha, it seemed, had brought Katish to see her that morning. They had eleven o'clock coffee in the garden and as they chatted pleasantly it had gradually become clear to Mother that Katish still thought that Mother had sent for her and that her belongings were out in front in the electric automobile! Aunt Martha blandly avoided Mother's eye while these amazing facts were sinking in; she knew that Mother, after breaking bread with Katish and hearing the Russian woman's delight in her beloved rose garden, could never deal her the hurt of sending her away.

Katish's English, though odd, had been sufficient to convey her gratitude in being offered this pleasant place to live and work. "Ai, is nice! I like!"

Mother was stymied and she knew it.

We had to admit that Katish did look jolly. She was a little one side or the other of thirty. Her short, sturdy figure, wide mouth, and snub nose in a round face gave her a look of cheerful reliability. But it was her dancing black eyes that fascinated us. They were large and perfectly round, and resembled the luscious black cherries that the grocer has polished to put in the very front of the window. You couldn't resist them.

And that Katish definitely could cook was immediately apparent.

"Gosh! I'll bet Aunt Martha didn't know that Katish was such a *good* cook!" Bub speculated unkindly as he bit into a piece of creamy cheese cake. "She probably thought she'd feed us on raw carrots and such junk." Bub's resentment had been considerably softened by Mother's announcement that he wouldn't have to go to dancing school any longer. Even Katish's small salary would make some adjustments necessary.

*Katish having coffee with
Mother and Aunt Martha*

The cheese cake that Bub munched so contentedly was the first we had ever tasted that did not have the regrettable texture of peanut butter. That cake was later to win Katish a proposal of marriage, much to Aunt Martha's chagrin. Here is the recipe; I have never found one to compare with it.

KATISH'S CHEESE CAKE

Cover the bottom of a spring form mold with 18 pieces of finely crushed zwieback mixed with 1½ tablespoons each of butter and sugar. Then cream 1 cup plus 2 tablespoons of sugar with 4 packages of Philadelphia cream cheese. Add 2 level tablespoons of flour, a pinch of salt, a 1-inch length of vanilla bean finely cut, and the beaten yolks of 4 eggs. Mix well and add 1 cup of sour cream. Fold in 4 stiffly beaten egg whites and pour into the crumb-lined pan. Bake in a moderate oven (350°) for about one hour. The crumb crust will be thin and crisp and the cake very light and creamy.

Katish was tremendously interested in everything she saw about her in this strange country and Bub and I were flattered when she came to us for explanations. On the first Saturday after she was installed in our kitchen I was delegated to take her into the city to shop for some equipment that our late departed cook had allowed to scorch beyond repair during moments of what must have been deep religious abstraction. Katish thoroughly enjoyed our ride in the streetcar. She surprised the harassed conductor by pausing to wish him a pleasant good-morning, and it seemed only natural for me to relinquish to her my usual seat next the window, for she found all the sights of the busy streets enchanting. But as the car approached the intersections with its bell clanging a raucous warning she would shut her eyes tightly. "*Boshe moi!* Is miracle we are alive!" she would exclaim with dramatic relief when we had passed safely through the skeins of interlocking traffic.

I took her to the housewares department of a large store and seeing her delight in the gleaming aluminum and gay pottery, I'm afraid I encouraged her to charge more than the minimum necessities to Mother's account. When we left the store, Katish turned and stood looking back into its busy aisles.

"There are thousands of people in the store at any hour of the day," I told her, seeking to impress. "Hundreds of clerks alone."

"So I am thinking," Katish answered anxiously. "But I am thinking, what happen if all people decide to go out at the same time?"

I had to admit that I didn't know. It might be pretty disastrous—something like a theatre fire. For a moment the idea was alarming. "But they never do," I reassured Katish and myself. "They just never want to. Let's go have a soda."

So we went into an Owl Drug Store and had chocolate sodas. Katish was fascinated. She had eaten frozen mousses in Russia and real ice cream in China, but she had never experienced the delight of a soda. At first she wasn't sure that it was proper for a grown-up person to suck up the liquid part through a straw. It seemed a childish thing to do. But the ticklish soda got up her nose and the lump of ice cream rose alarmingly to the top of the glass when she tilted it. She picked up the straws and followed my example, and a smile of pure bliss overspread her friendly face. Sucking happily, she nodded her approval at me over the glass and her conversion to the ice cream soda was complete. She decided that the American drug store was a really wonderful institution when she found that she could buy there an article of kitchen equipment that the housewares department hadn't been able to supply.

When we reached home I went into the kitchen with Katish to see what we were going to have for dinner. Since we children were at home for a hot lunch on Saturdays, Mother had established the custom of a light supper in the evening. "What are we having, Katish?" I inquired with interest, since an ice cream soda is merely an appetizer to a thirteen-year-old.

"We have mushrooms and ham and the fine salad." Katish brought out a big basket of mushrooms looking like so many miniature umbrellas fashioned of creamy, delicate silk.

"No dessert!" I yelped in greedy protest, forgetting to express my appreciation of the mushrooms.

"Well, maybe kissel, if no bread and jam now." Katish shook an admonitory finger. It hadn't taken her long to learn that Bub and I could do with a snack at any hour. But we were pleased that she never said anything foolish about spoiling our appetites for dinner. We had the fine, ferocious appetites of healthy adolescents, and spoiling them was next to impossible.

Her delectable hot sandwiches of mushrooms in sour cream over thin slices of ham were superb, if temporary, appeasement.

MUSHROOMS IN SOUR CREAM

Wash 1 pound of mushrooms quickly. Never, never let mushrooms stand in water. Cut off the stems just where they cease to be woody; but do not peel. Slice each cap from the top down through the stalk. Heat 3 tablespoons of butter in a heavy pan. When pan and butter are hot, but not burning, put in a layer of the mushrooms. Don't overcrowd the pan and don't bruise the mushrooms with rough stirring; if you do these things the juice will run out and boil away. When the first lot of mushrooms is delicately browned, remove them from the pan, heat a little more fat if necessary, and brown another layer. When all the slices are nicely browned, stir 2 tablespoons of flour into the fat remaining in the pan. Add 1½ cups of milk and stir to form a smooth sauce. Return all the mushrooms to the pan, stir in ½ cup of sour cream, salt and pepper to taste, and add 3 or 4 drops of Maggi Seasoning. Cook over low heat for five or six minutes. Used sparingly, Maggi Seasoning points up the flavor of mushrooms, but too much of it will give a flavor of dried mushrooms.

MUSHROOM AND HAM SANDWICHES

Prepare a thin slice of buttered toast for each serving. Over the toast place a thin slice of delicately flavored baked or boiled ham which has been quickly sautéed in a little butter or ham fat. Then pour over each serving a generous amount of bubbling hot mushrooms in sour cream.

Katish had prepared a large basket of the mushrooms and not all of them would be needed for that night's supper. We were to learn that a generous jar of these mushrooms in sour cream in the icebox was a stand-by of Katish's cuisine. Like most Russians, Katish felt that hospitality was a spontaneous thing. She would have been greatly wounded if ever Mother had been forced to say, "I do wish we could have urged the Smiths to stay to dinner, but I just don't know what we could have given them." Katish always had something on hand for unexpected guests and she accomplished it without extravagance or waste.

The mushrooms in sour cream would keep for days and their subtly delicious flavor enhanced and extended a number of dishes to elegance and abundance. If the larder was really low Katish might hard-boil an egg for each person. Then she would open up a can of shrimp or lobster or boned chicken. She would split the eggs in half lengthwise and arrange them in a shallow casserole with the seafood or chicken, then pour the mushrooms over and heat in a moderate oven. With a big salad, this made a meal. Or she might give us the mushrooms hot and savory on tiny circles of toast as a starting course for a light meal. This is one of the best ways to use them. They are worthy of a place by themselves and a receptive palate.

The kissel that Katish promised me is a very common Russian dessert, served alike to children and sophisticates. It is made of fruit juice thickened with potato starch. Some types of juice benefit for adult tastes by the addition of a little good brandy or port. With a few cans of fruit juice in the pantry it can be made up in five minutes' time.

KISSEL

Apricot, apple, loganberry, and raspberry juice all make excellent kissel. For each cup of juice, use about 2 teaspoons of potato starch.

Moisten the starch with a little of the juice and put the remaining juice into a saucepan over a low fire. Stir in enough sugar to sweeten, but take care not to overdo it. When the fruit juice and sugar mixture comes to a boil, stir in the moistened potato starch. Stir briskly for a minute or two and take from the fire. Chill thoroughly before serving.

A spoonful of brandy stirred into apricot juice after it has been taken from the fire is delicious. Or you may use the brandy to flavor whipped cream to be served with the dessert.

Bottled apple juice makes a wonderful kissel when it is combined with an equal quantity of port and a teaspoon of finely grated lemon peel.

Katish took particular delight in preparing the big wooden bowls of green salad that we had almost every night. Never in her life had she seen such gorgeous displays of fruits and vegetables as those of the California markets. Oranges, great globes of purest gold, were banked in a lavish splendor that was breathtaking to one who had been accustomed to regard them as a special Christmas treat. Jade-green cabbages and royal-purple eggplants vied in beauty with more exotic vegetables such as delicate avocados, artichokes like great close-hearted emerald flowers, and, in early summer, fat tender spears of asparagus.

A smile of wonder came over Katish's piquant features as she viewed this abundance. "Ai, Paradise has been given to the Americantzi," she breathed.

But Katish refused to be dazzled when it came to making her purchases. The market men soon learned that only the freshest and best of their beautiful wares could get into Katish's basket. Mother had suggested that Katish telephone for supplies, but that proved to be more involved than Mother had counted on. Katish's English often needed the aid of her expressive hands and eyes to be comprehensible, for at first she could not remember the American names of all the fruits and vegetables. And besides, she didn't want to be cheated of that delightful daily excursion. It was some distance from our house to the shopping center, and the only car in the family at that time was a deplorable, cut-down affair known as The Menace, and belonging to Bub. This unreliable chariot was not always available.

Katish took the difficulty in stride. "*Nitchevo.* It is nothing. I go on my foot." And so she did.

She displayed a mind of her own when it came to selecting foods and planning menus. Mother solved the problem of a suitable budget by giving her a certain sum of money at the beginning of each week and letting her spend it as she thought best. It wasn't a large sum, but hardly a month was to pass without Katish's appearing with a present that she had bought for Mother with the money she had saved. It never seemed to occur to either of them that she might have returned the money instead. Katish loved giving presents and Mother loved getting them, so that was that.

A thing we'd better get straight right away, if we're going to understand each other and Katish, is just what is the sour cream she used in preparing so many of her fine dishes. Katish's horror knew no bounds when she ordered it days ahead of time from our grocer and then found that the well-meaning but benighted soul had simply put aside a bottle of fresh cream to sour for her! Sour cream is especially prepared and packaged at the dairy. When properly fresh, it has a very delicate sour taste, and none of the unpleasant odor of stale cream. It is thick, almost as thick as whipped cream, and much more delicious. One very good use for the uncooked sour cream (*smetana* is the Russian word for it) that we learned from Katish is as a condiment for snappy radishes. You dip the radish in sour cream and then in salt, and it is really very good. Americans look surprised when Russians put butter on their radishes; but it's all right, they only do this when sour cream isn't offered!

Among Americans it is usually safer to refer to sour cream by some euphemism. Katish simply called it Russian cream after one or two disappointing encounters with timid souls.

One of the splendid recipes in which Katish used sour cream was her Beef Stroganoff, a scrumptious concoction of many virtues. It can be prepared ahead of time; it makes a wonderful pièce de résistance for buffet or sit-down dinner, and while it is simple enough for family meals, it is grand enough for any company.

BEEF STROGANOFF

Sauté ½ pound of sliced mushrooms in butter or other fat. Put them aside and brown 1 large onion, sliced, in the fat. Set the onions aside, put some more fat into the pan and make sure it is good and hot. Have 1½ pounds of round steak ready to go into the hot frying pan. First, have your butcher cut the steak about ½ inch thick. Then take a sharp knife and cut the steak into very thin strips, about 1½ to 2½ inches in length. Toss the strips in flour, salt, and pepper. Then drop them into the sizzling, fat-coated frying pan. Don't put in too much meat at one time, for you want it to brown quickly without drying out. When all the meat is nicely browned, sprinkle 2 tablespoons of flour into the pan and blend it with the remaining drippings, browning it well. Then add 2 cups of water slowly, stirring to form a smooth gravy. Use just a little brown meat extract to give a rich color. Put meat, mushrooms, and onions into the sauce, cover tightly, and cook until the meat is tender. Leave over a low top flame, or put into a moderate oven in a serving casserole. Ten minutes before serving, stir in ⅔ cup of sour cream, adjust seasoning, shake in 3 or 4 drops of Maggi Seasoning. Serve with French fried or fluffy mashed potatoes.

We all, even Mother, had been a little afraid that with a cook so foreign we should have to dine every night on exotic dishes. But Katish proved immediately that she knew well how to deal with such staples as chops, steaks, and roasts. Somewhere in the second-hand shops of Los Angeles she had unearthed a Russian-American cook book, and armed with a dictionary, she explored the mysteries of fried chicken, waffles, and others of our favorite recipes.

Her lamb chops were a revelation. She would have them cut

very thick, one to a person. First she seasoned them ever so lightly with a cut clove of garlic, liberally with salt and pepper. She put them into the broiler with the fat side up, and rather close to the flame. When the fat had browned and run down over the sides of the chops, she cooked them on one side, then on the other, browning them to perfection. Small thick steaks she treated in the same way. And always she seasoned her meats so carefully that they needed no addition at table. Salt and pepper were rubbed into meat and even into bone. The pepper was invariably freshly ground from a little wooden French mill. Katish maintained that meat seasoned in cooking had a more wonderful aroma, and further, that a great deal of pleasure was lost if the first bite of food was disappointing. If one had to turn to one's neighbor at table and politely request the salt, and then wait for it to be passed (it must, by all means, said Katish, be set down between hands, to avoid passing bad luck) before beginning to enjoy the food upon one's plate, the cook had failed at the start.

Fortunately, Katish's talents did not run exclusively to expensive things. No, she loved creating masterpieces from inexpensive ingredients. "Good steak is thanks to butcher," she declared modestly. "But the good cutlets thanks to cook. I show." The term cutlet, to a Russian, has a different meaning from ours, as you will see.

KATISH'S BEEF OR VEAL CUTLETS

Take 1 pound of good quality ground beef or veal; have the butcher leave a little fat on the meat when he grinds it. Into a mixing bowl put 3 average slices of French bread, or 2 slices of the ready sliced variety of plain white bread. Remove all crusts. Pour a cup of water over the bread and let it stand for a few minutes. Or use half water and half dry red wine. When the bread is well soaked, beat it into a paste with the water. Don't squeeze out or discard any of the water or wine. Put in 2 tablespoons of finely chopped onion, 2 teaspoons of salt, a goodly grinding of black pepper. Then add the beef or veal and mix well. You will have a mixture that is quite moist. Wet your hands in cold water and shape the meat into flat cakes. Roll the cakes in fine dry bread crumbs. Let them stand in a cool place until five minutes before serving time. Then heat some fat in a heavy iron frying pan. Have it piping hot when you put the cutlets in. Fry them quickly on one side, then on the other. The cakes should not be thick, so that they will cook through in the time that it takes for a crispy, deep brown crust to form on the outside. They will be light and tender and running with savory juice when your fork cuts into them. Serve them with spicy Russian mustard. (The type known as Bahamian mustard is very similar.) Or serve a brown gravy, passed separately. One pound of meat will make 12 to 14 cutlets.

Good cooks, as a rule, are good-natured people. Katish lived up to this rule, but now and then she was upset and bewildered by the teasing of tradespeople and delivery boys. The iceman, struck by her cheery countenance, affectionately and impudently christened her Buttercup. For some reason that he could not understand, this annoyed Katish. If she saw him coming, she would flounce out of the kitchen at his approach. "Hi, Buttercup," he would shout then, "why are you running away?" His loud foolery could be heard all through the house. That was even worse. So Katish stuck to her kitchen and bore it, but she could not grin. It was a long time before any of us discovered why she minded so much to be called by the name of this gay little field flower.

One day, just after the disturbing visit of the iceman, Bub found her muttering to herself. "Calling me butter dish, just for that I am not thin like stick," she fumed audibly. "But I not wish to be like stick."

With a whoop Bub confronted her. "Katish! Is that why you hate being called Buttercup? Oh, how funny!"

"How you think funny? Do you wish to be named after dish?" Katish whirled on Bub. "You pretty round, also."

"But it hasn't a thing to do with roundness or dishes!" Bub explained between shouts of laughter. "A buttercup is a pretty yel-

"Butter dish!"

low flower. I'm sure the iceman calls you that because you look so sunny."

Katish was somewhat mollified, but she never got to like that iceman and no one ever gave him the satisfaction of knowing that she had thought that a buttercup was some sort of butter dish.

CHAPTER TWO

The strangeness of American customs and what our genial Russian cook called the "unreasonful" English language might have proved a real handicap to a less hardy soul in matching wits for the first time with the wide-awake American businessman, but Katish was not easily daunted. Not for nothing had she made her way halfway around the world, alone, and almost penniless. She was a mellow blend of realist and philosopher, and she did not hesitate to achieve her ends by a cheerful, almost naïve indirection that sometimes left Mother breathless.

For a short time Katish enjoyed going from one huge, colorful market to another, comparing merchandise and prices. The drive-in markets that were beginning to flourish in California in the twenties were an institution that truly earned the favorite adjectives of Hollywood—colossal, magnificent, stupendous. Katish was impressed and, at first, a little confused. But it did not take her long to decide that the old European practice of trading in one place and creating there as much influence as one could was the best method in the long run. Finally her choice fell upon an older market which had only partially succumbed to the furor for glamour.

There was less chromium and tile about the place than others boasted, but it was clean, its wares good, and the help obliging.

One day Mother and I were buying fruit in this market when we caught a sentence in Katish's bumpy English. It came from the direction of the butcher's counter. The sound of her first words stopped us in our tracks, fascinated and utterly incapable of remembering that eavesdropping is not a very nice thing to do. For she was talking about us. And to our mystification, she was painting a pretty grand picture, quite out of proportion to our modest circumstances. We finally turned and walked silently out of the market, feeling that the clerks ought to bow low as we passed, and that nothing less than a sixteen-cylinder motor should await us at the curb. A tremor of suppressed horror shook Mother as her reluctant eye fell once more on the boasts and quips chalked gaudily on the three fenders and solitary door of my brother's adored cut-down.

"What's the matter?" Bub asked. "You two look as if you'd seen something—and you aren't saying a word!" he finished in amazement.

"You should have heard the things Katish was telling the butcher about us," Mother gasped.

"What kind of things?"

"Well, we're frightfully rich, for one thing," Mother revealed. "And a very important family. I didn't quite make out whether we're in politics or something artistic. But anyone who is anyone at all knows the name. And only the very best will do for us."

"Did the butcher believe it?" Bub wanted to know.

"Katish was awfully convincing," Mother admitted.

"Hot dog!" exclaimed Bub. "I know some people I'll have to get Katish to talk to."

"Drive right back to the market when you've dropped us," Mother ordered. "Katish will have a lot of things to carry, and I can't wait to talk to her."

Mother controlled her impatience until Katish had taken off her outdoor things and gone to work on the dinner. Then she sauntered out to the kitchen and indulged in some highly irrelevant conversation. Something about the cold chicken in the icebox. Rather embarrassed, she finally explained that we had happened to over-hear some of what Katish had been saying to the butcher. She was a little puzzled, Mother admitted. Did Katish think it was quite right to go about misleading people like that?

Katish was not fazed. "But Amerikantzi so democratic!" she exclaimed in reasonable tones which said that now Mother must understand perfectly.

But she didn't understand. "I still don't see, Katish, why you should tell such stories to the tradespeople."

"But you see, with such democracy, when I tell to butcher that I am working for important family, very rich and so famous, then he does not mind that I am myself cook. *He is much* polite, and he gives the very fine meat." With a pleased look she displayed the neat cubes of stewing beef, richly red and thinly marbled with creamy fat, that she had just obtained.

Mother shook her head helplessly. When she decided to let Aunt Martha enjoy the story, our aunt looked thoughtful and said slowly, "Well, you know, it is true that Uncle Frank invented a number of things, though I must say that I never understood any of them very well, and then, there were all those books Grandfather wrote. Per-haps you needn't be too firm about it."

Mother laughed and then sighed and I knew she was thinking of all the money it had cost the family to publish Grandfather's books and obtain Uncle Frank's patents. We all enjoyed the stew that Katish gave us that night, and no more was said about misleading the storekeepers.

KATISH'S BEEF OR VEAL STEW

For each pound of meat take 1 medium onion. Slice the onion and brown it lightly in butter or other good fat. Put the onion aside and brown ¼ pound of sliced mushrooms for each pound of meat. When the mushrooms are a lovely brown, put them aside with the onions on a piece of brown paper to drain. Trim the beef or veal and cut it into 1½ inch chunks or cubes. Salt, pepper, and flour it evenly and brown it in more of the hot fat. (When Katish says to brown meat, do it well, seeing that all sides receive a beautiful deep coat. In perfect browning lies one of the cardinal differences between a perfect stew and a mediocre one). Then pour on enough boiling water to cover the meat. Return the onion slices to the pan and simmer tightly covered for about one hour, adding more water if necessary. Fifteen minutes before serving time, make sure that there is enough water in the pan for a goodly amount of gravy, thicken it to the desired consistency with a little moistened flour. Add enough brown meat extract to give a fine color and stir in a half cup of sour cream. Then put in the mushroom slices, adjust the seasoning, shake in 3 or 4 drops of Maggi Seasoning; cover the pot and simmer very gently for fifteen minutes. You may add small new potatoes to the pot in time to cook tender or serve with mashed potatoes. But save your carrots, turnips, and even peas—unless they be ever so tiny and fresh from the garden—for another day, please!

Katish often served dishes that she called stews, but on a restaurant menu they would be more likely to appear under the expensive French dishes with a name ending in *aux champignons*. For Katish wasn't going to have any carrots or turnips cluttering up her stews—an attitude in which we heartily concurred. A separately cooked vegetable is infinitely preferable. In those days vitamins weren't on every tongue, but somehow we seemed to consume as many vegetables as people do today. A huge bowl of simple green salad seemed then—and still does—the perfect accompaniment to stew.

In recent years I have found a very good use for one of Katish's very Russian recipes—pelmeny. These little shell-shaped morsels of noodle dough and well-seasoned meat are greatly liked by most Russians, but Americans often find them heavy when served in sufficient quantities for an entree. Ordinarily, they are boiled in a rich bouillon and served with sour cream and a sprinkling of fresh dill. But I have discovered that they make irresistible tidbits when fried in butter, stuck on colored picks, and served sizzling hot with the dry martinis. Dry martinis and the atmosphere of an American cocktail party are in strange contrast to the story that Katish related when she first made pelmeny for us.

Once, during her childhood, Katish told us, her family had made a long trip through Siberia in the dead of winter. Her father, a priest, was going to fill the post of a superior who was ill in a village many miles from their home. They traveled through the still, deep winter snows in sleighs, stopping at night at primitive stations that provided meager shelter for travelers, and a stable for tired horses. Most of their food they had to take with them. Katish's mother had made up bags and bags of pelmeny and put them outside to freeze solid before leaving home. Each night when they reached their stopping place on the journey, she would take out a bag of pelmeny and put them to boil in the steaming water that she found in the station samovar. Or she would fry them in some of the frozen butter that they had also brought in the sleigh. Katish would smile as she remembered how good the hot pelmeny had tasted to the cold, hungry little family.

A feature of this story that was most thrilling to me was the fact that somehow as they traveled through the dusky, white-blanketed forests one afternoon, Katish's baby brother had fallen from the sleigh. Sound asleep, and well wrapped, he gave no cry, and no one missed him. On they went, through the shadowy forest. Then suddenly, with deep terror, the mother missed the precious bundle. Frantically they turned the sleigh in the narrow track, and whipping up the weary horses, sped back along the way they had come, driver, father, mother, and Katish all straining tensely into the gloom to catch sight of the baby. For there were wolves, they knew, in the forest. At last, after an agonizing ten minutes, they came across the baby, unharmed and still snugly wrapped, lying on his back in the rutted road and howling with reassuring lustiness.

"He only hungry; that why he cry," Katish finished her tale comfortably as she rolled dough to paper thinness for our first pelmeny.

PELMENY

Beat a large, whole egg until frothy, then sift in 2 cups of flour and 2 teaspoons of salt; add sufficient warm water to make a soft dough. Knead gently, then cover with a cloth to keep from drying out, and let the dough stand ten minutes to "rest." Knead again until very smooth. Roll out quite thin on a floured board, and cut in small circles, not more than 1½ inches in diameter! On each circle put a teaspoon of the following filling: ½ pound ground beef, salt and freshly ground pepper to taste, 1 teaspoon finely chopped fresh dill, 1 tablespoon grated onion. Mix well. Fold over the circles of dough and press together well around the edges. Then take hold of the "corners" of the resulting half circles and pull them together and press well. The pelmeny will now look rather like some small, intriguing sea shells. Unless you can work quickly, roll out only a part of your dough at one time, for if it dries, the edges of the shells will come apart in cooking.

You may boil the pelmeny in bouillon, drain them, and serve with sour cream and a sprinkling of chopped dill or chives. But they will be truly sensational if you fry them in butter and serve them on wooden picks with cocktails. You can make them up days ahead and put them to freeze in the refrigerator trays to be ready for the event. This will be less picturesque than Katish's mother's method of putting the pelmeny out of doors to freeze, but it will be eminently satisfactory. And it wouldn't be a bad idea to arrange a sleigh ride to precede the martinis and pelmeny!

Ours was an informal house, and Katish had not been with us long before we regarded her as a real friend. On rainy days, and on occasions when Bub and I were being "punished" for some crimes natural to our years by being shut in the house, we would wander out to the kitchen to visit with Katish. She was glad to see us, for she greatly loved children.

We had a part-time gardener, an eldery Italian named Julio. He was lazy and dirty and often drunk, but he had a genius with flowers. Katish had no use at all for Julio, but he found good use for her.

In spite of the fact that he was in his sixties, his wife yearly presented him with a fine bambino. It was necessary for his wife to work between confinements in order to provide for the little ones here and to come. Sometimes there was no one at home to look after the babies and then Julio would bring two or three of the youngest for a little "visit" with Katish.

She adored the big-eyed, dirty infants, and the moment Julio deposited them in her kitchen she would begin to work like a trooper to get them scrubbed, patched, loved, and fed before he came to take them back to their customary squalor.

Julio's drunken laziness brought down her scorn and wrath upon his far from humble head. It only seemed to amuse him when she scolded him for his neglect of the adorable bambinos. But babies came too easily to Julio to be valued. He would lean against the kitchen wall and laugh as Katish admonished him. When she grew angry he would put a finger to his tongue, then reach out and touch Katish. "Psssst!" he would hiss, as a hot iron does when it is tried with a wet finger. Slyly he would point at her and repeat the hissing noise, making fun of her righteous anger, until she could bear no more, and would tell him to take his newly scrubbed babies and go.

Even Bub and I, big as we were, received a large share of her warm maternal solicitude. She would amuse us with stories and comfort us with good things to eat when we were confined to the house for our misdoings. Once Bub and I had made up our minds that we could leave Aunt Martha's treachery out of it and take Katish on her own merits, we began to love her. When Katish admitted that perhaps Aunt Martha was "having too much personality," we were delighted. Her loyalty led her to declare that a neighbor who sometimes objected to the noise we children and our friends made, was not "well-refined." She never minded when we laughed at her mistakes, and happily took advantage of the opportunity to learn the proper expression.

Because she confused Bub with Bob, my brother received a new name. I had always been Sis and my brother Bub. We had Aunt Martha to blame for our practically nameless state. For years before we had been born, Mother had promised our aunt the privilege of naming the offspring that she firmly intended to have in due time and God willing. It had seemed a small thing, Mother said, to promise one who had been recently blighted by the loss of the only lover who seemed likely ever to aspire to the heart of so imperious a maiden. And Aunt Martha had grimly exacted fulfillment when the time came, with the result that the names which she inscribed in the family Bible were, so far as we had anything to say about it, interred there forever. They just wouldn't bear the light of day— but the fact that she had had in mind the matchless gem of a name Waldo DeVere, for a second boy, when and if he ever put in his appearance, will give you an idea of her talents along this line. It may have been this that made Mother feel two children were enough, since she was a woman who kept her promises.

My brother was overjoyed when we all adopted Katish's version of the outgrown Bub, and he became Bob forever after.

Aunt Martha had not entirely relinquished her interest in Katish now that she was safely installed in our household. "I know how easygoing you are, Mary, and I feel responsible for sending Katish to you," she would say. There was that itching sense of responsibility again! Off she would go on a tour of inspection of the house. It was seldom that she could find anything to complain of in Katish's housekeeping or cooking. But she could complain, perhaps with some fairness, that Katish was inclined to spoil us children. Katish took this interference placidly, for she never forgot that it had indeed been Aunt Martha who had brought her to Mother. When our aunt began one of her lectures, Mother and Katish would exchange a half-smile and then attend very seriously as long as it lasted.

When Aunt Martha had done, Katish would bring out tea and perhaps some of her marvelous strawberry jam, and peace would descend. Mother usually served tea in the afternoon if there were visitors, but Katish had tea at least five times a day. It is really a wonder that the Russians have not long ago drunk up all the tea in China, for their appetites for it are insatiable. The expression which means *to drink tea* has by much use been welded into a single word. *Tchai* is tea; *pit* is to drink. *Tchaipit* has grown to be one word!

KATISH'S HEAVENLY STRAWBERRY JAM

Wash, drain, and pick over 4 cups of strawberries. Use only perfect or nearly perfect berries and cut away any bad spots; but leave the berries whole otherwise. Put them into a large kettle and cover with 5 cups of sugar. Let them stand three hours. Then put over a low fire. Bring to a boil and continue boiling for just eight minutes. Then add ½ cup of lemon juice and boil just two minutes longer. Let cool a little, skim and stir to prevent the berries from coming to the top. Pour into sterile jars and seal. This makes the most beautiful and wonderfully flavored strawberry jam in the world.

One custom attributed to Russians irked Katish considerably. It is the widespread calumny that Russians put jam in their tea. Katish indignantly maintained that she had never seen a countryman do such a shocking thing. As a mild form of parlor sport I have carried on her search for just one Russian who would show such a lack of respect for his national beverage. I must admit that I've never found my man, though I've had fine opportunities for research, since I took Katish's excellent advice many years ago and married a Russian. (Katish couldn't bear to think that her efforts in teaching me all her best dishes would be wasted.)

Another rather amusing misapprehension is the fairly general conviction among the uninitiated that tea comes out of a samovar. As a matter of fact, only boiling water ever properly emerges from the great, round-bellied brass or silver vessel. The tea, a very strong infusion, is made in the small smug pot that warms its fat sides on top of the samovar. The boiling water from the large vessel is used to dilute this strong infusion to the desired strength. To heat the water, the center well of the samovar is filled with charcoal. Should the charcoal prove refractory, a soft leather riding boot is slipped over the vessel and pumped up and down briskly like a bellows until a fine glow results—at least that is said to be the old army method, and it works!

Katish
making
Tea – Russian style

Katish marveled that in a climate like California's people exhibited so much energy. Why, she wondered, did not everyone relax and spend his days sleeping in the glorious sun? The hustle and bustle that was everywhere seemed strangely out of place to one who had known a more leisurely way of life. The mischief we children managed to get into amazed her.

One of our repeated misdeeds was that of climbing on the roof. This we were strictly forbidden to do, but now and then Bob and some of his friends would climb into the branches of a huge eucalyptus tree that stood close to the house and thence to the roof. Unwilling to be outdone by mere boys, I would follow. But unfortunately I was terrified of heights. When I had got a few feet above the ground, my head would begin to whirl and my stomach to churn. Green, but unbeaten, I would climb on until I had achieved the comparative safety of the chimney. There I would crouch, shaking and sick, and hoping that the boys wouldn't notice that I didn't join in their reckless tripping along the ridgepole. For a time the hardihood of the very young saw me through, and I managed to crawl miserably back down the tree when the time came. But suddenly, one day, every vestige of courage deserted me, and I clung, wailing disgracefully, to the wide chimney. I just could not force myself to climb and slide down the slippery branches of the eucalyptus. Hooting joyfully at a silly girl's cowardice, Bob and his friends deserted me there. And there I stayed, weeping and shaking with terror until I heard a low voice, close by. "Do not be afraid, *golubka* (little dove). Comes Katish."

Over the edge of the roof appeared Katish's loyal, sympathetic face. Pulling herself up to the top of the long ladder she had brought and propped precariously against the side of the house, she held out a hand to me. Sniffing and tearful, I grasped that hand and edged to the ladder. Then slowly Katish waddled backward and downward and I crawled after her. As we neared the haven of solid ground, Aunt Martha drove up, bringing Mother home from a bridge party. My aunt was so astounded by the sight of Katish's plump figure descending from the roof that she forgot to look where she was going and ran up over the curb and into our lawn. They jumped from the car and ran to us in time to steady the ladder for our last uncertain steps.

"You should have left the foolish child up there until she had learned her lesson, Katish," Aunt Martha scolded when she had heard our account of events. "It's disgraceful for those youngsters to carry on the way they do."

Katish kept a protective arm around me. "Poor *golubka*, Katish take care," she kept murmuring comfortingly.

"Stay with Katish for the rest of the afternoon," Mother ordered diplomatically. "I'll have a talk with your brother when he comes in."

Gladly I kept to the warmth and security of Katish's kitchen for the rest of the day. Roof climbing was in the future omitted from our list of childish crimes.

In the late afternoon the kitchen was filled with soothing smells and sounds. There would be the low "chuk-chuk" of something simmering in a pot on the back of the stove, and spicy or savory odors would drift from the oven when Katish opened the door.

One of the good things that provided energy for our mischief was what Katish called marinated ribs of beef. To Americans, they would be barbecued shortribs, but to Katish the barbecue was an unknown institution.

MARINATED SHORTRIBS

Have your butcher cut 3 pounds of beef shortribs into serving pieces. Wipe the meat with a damp cloth and pack it into a deep bowl and pour over it this marinade: Mix together 2 tablespoons of hot Russian mustard, 3 teaspoons of salt, a good amount of black pepper, ½ teaspoon chili powder, ½ teaspoon sugar, 1 tablespoon lemon juice, and 6 tablespoons olive oil. Shake up well with a crushed clove of garlic. Then pour it over the meat and wedge a few thick slices of onion between the pieces of beef. Cover and keep in a cool place for from eight to twenty-four hours, stirring now and then. Put the ribs into a roasting pan, leaving excess sauce and onion slices aside. Brown the meat at a high temperature for about fifteen minutes. Turn the fire low and cover the pan. After forty-five minutes, put the onion and remaining marinade into the pan. Cover again. An hour later, remove cover and brown the onions and let the fat on the beef crisp up a little. Serve these ribs with baked potatoes and pass a dish of your favorite barbecue sauce, or gravy made from the drippings.

Another hearty and inexpensive main dish that we liked was Katish's spare ribs with bread stuffing. It is delicious and makes a little meat go a long way. When Katish first tasted American bread stuffing in a restaurant she found it depressing fare. But it did seem to have possibilities that appealed to her thrifty, inventive soul. With the aid of cook book, dictionary, and imagination, she worked out her own recipe.

SPARERIBS WITH STUFFING

Select a good-sized, meaty cut of spareribs. Rub the ribs well with garlic, flour, salt, and pepper. Make some of Katish's bread stuffing and roll it inside the ribs. Put it into a hot oven to brown, then cover and cook slowly for an hour and a half. Make a rich brown gravy with the drippings in the pan.

BREAD STUFFING

There is no very exact recipe for Katish's bread stuffing, but there are several things about it that make it distinctly good and different. First, the slightly stale bread is crumbled to about the size of small marbles—never smaller than large peas. Then, the bread must not be all of one kind. Use a few slices of white bread, one or two of whole-wheat, a slice of French or crusty Italian bread, and do try to have two or three squares of cornbread, or cornmeal muffins. You will get a very superior flavor and texture if you follow these rules. Fry a large onion, fairly finely chopped, to a delicious brown in plenty of bacon fat. Put aside to drain. Moisten—do not wet—the bread and mix it up together, but don't squeeze or squash it into a mushy mass. Fry it to a good brown in more of the bacon drippings. Turn and stir it frequently until it is thoroughly browned. Then put in the onions, salt and pepper to taste (and do taste), just a little sage and thyme. Don't overdo these seasonings unless you have a hopeless passion for them. Moisten the stuffing a little if it seems very dry, but again—don't have it wet. It will get a lot of flavorsome drippings from the pork ribs.

This same stuffing is excellent for a stuffed shoulder of pork or veal or lamb. With veal, a few sautéed mushroom slices are a fine addition. For duckling, use largely whole-wheat bread, add a handful of seedless raisins, and a generous quantity of chopped walnut meats. Every last forkful will disappear.

When we had roast duckling, Katish would make a thrifty extra bowl of the stuffing and cook it in a loose mound in the pan beside the fowl. It would grow brown and crusty on the outside in the drippings. There is not a great deal of meat on a duck, but we always had a second-day dish made by heating this stuffing in a casserole with a layer of shredded meat removed from the carcass and gravy made from the left-over drippings. It was excellent.

It was not difficult for Katish to adapt her own ideas of good food to those of an American family. The principles of good cooking are universal and Russians are a naturally flexible people with a great willingness to admire and emulate the good things of other countries, while retaining enough of the individuality of their own ways to add just a titillating spice of unfamiliarity.

More often than not our dinners consisted of only one or two dishes, but those dishes were always superbly made, and Katish knew it and was frankly proud of her handiwork. Her black eyes would sparkle with equal pride over a perfect, but simple and inexpensive, casserole, and one of her fabulous babas au rhum. She had only scorn for ostentatious simplicity and showy extravagance alike.

When we laughed over the scene in *The Gold Rush* where Charlie Chaplin boils his shoe for nourishment, Katish laughed too. But she told us, "In Russia, after the revolution, you would have had to make the shoe before you could boil it."

And then she told us a wonderful tale about the remarkable shoes of friends of hers, a young Russian couple living frugally in New York, and earning their way by hard work through a university. The couple longed for exercise and recreation in the little time that was left from their studies and work. When a kindly American offered them the use of his private tennis court, and even considerately undertook to supply them with racquets, they were delighted. White flannels were desirable, but they could be dispensed with, for their host knew their circumstances; tennis shoes were all they would need to buy.

As they walked one day through the lower East Side, they paused before a shop window filled with many and wondrous things. There, peeking out from a pile of glass and silver ornaments, were canvas shoes, only slightly dusty. What a wonderful opportunity to buy the needed tennis shoes at a saving that, though probably small, was important to them! They promptly made their wants known to the proprietor of the shop and came out elated with their luck, the parcels under their arms.

The next Saturday afternoon they went to play on the court. A number of people came in while they played. At first the newcomers seemed to pay no more than ordinary attention to the young Russians' game. But gradually they became aware that the Americans were taking a tremendous and embarrassingly personal interest in them. Obviously, they were filled with a mirth that was almost too much for them to contain. When Katish's young friends had finished their set, they determined to ask the cause of the bystanders' amusement.

"You honestly don't know, then?" a middle-aged man in the group marveled.

"No. If we knew the cause of your amusement, we should not ask."

The American looked a little shamefaced, but he could not repress a smile as he explained. "Well, I'll tell you. You see, I'm an undertaker myself or I probably wouldn't have known any better than you. But those shoes you are wearing are burial shoes for the dead. Their makers had in mind a light tripping over fleecy clouds, rather than the punishment you've been giving them. Better see to your feet, and take care of any blisters as soon as you can," he advised kindly.

"I knew something was wrong," the Russian girl admitted. "They are so flimsy and my feet do feel scraped. But how funny!" Then she and all the others burst into unrestrained laughter.

Stuffed-shirt simplicity didn't stand a chance with Katish and her friends.

CHAPTER THREE

Mother, like a good many other people, felt that Prohibition was a mistake. Moreover, it was a mistake in very bad taste. One did best to ignore it as far as possible. She was fortunate enough to have an old family doctor and friend who willingly supplied prescriptions for the modest amounts of port, sherry, and brandy that stocked our medicine cabinet. Since we were the sort of family that is never ill, she saw no harm in appropriating these stocks for kitchen use on special occasions. Katish justified these goings-on by stating firmly that such use was, in a way, medicinal. Like the apple a day—I suppose.

Katish hadn't been with us long before she learned that Julio, our weekly gardener, produced not only matchless dahlias and adorable bambinos, but "the ver' besta red wine in alla the California." Katish didn't know just how a respectable woman wanting a little wine to cook with could go about sampling the wares of the undoubtedly numerous bootleggers of Southern California, so she decided to take Julio's word for the excellence of his product. Thereafter Julio was wont to sidle up to the kitchen door occasionally with a suspicious bulge under his dirty old coat. Bob and I used to creep up behind him when we could and scare the life out of the old sinner with a whisper of "Cops!"

Mother felt a trifle doubtful about the wine, even though it was going to be cooked before it reached the table. Hadn't she heard that some of these amateur bootleggers used their bathtubs in the production of illicit liquor? It didn't seem probable that even Prohibition had hastened the process of wine making so that it could be conveniently fitted in between one Saturday night and the next. Katish offered reassurance in the statement that she was sure the gardener's family had never committed the indiscretion of using their tub for its normal purpose. A visiting friend, somewhat better informed, explained that it was gin, not wine, that was made in bathtubs.

It is amusing to remember the airy disdain with which Mother and Katish regarded this particular law of the land. For in many ways they were both distinctly strait-laced. Neither had succumbed to the modern style for short hair. They said it was a fad. The liberal use of make-up, so prevalent in the twenties, they found distressingly vulgar. Mother never owned a lipstick. Before coming down to dinner she would sometimes lightly rouge her cheeks. Then she would take up a square of old linen and vigorously rub her face until not a vestige of the artificial color remained. But the rubbing brought out a glow that satisfied Mother and made her feel she was being a little daring.

In our early teens Bob and I, like all of our generation, were inclined to show a faintly superior amusement at the undue restraint of our elders. When Mother suffered a broken arm because of what was to us an incomprehensible modesty, Katish's explanations were totally impotent to penetrate the fog of our bewilderment.

"Oh, well, grown-ups—" we finally said with a shrug and left it there. But I don't think we were any more dazed than the poor insurance salesman who precipitated the accident.

Mother, it seems, had been reading a novel on the living room sofa when Katish, thinking that she was upstairs, let the insurance man in without warning. At his approach, Mother had fled in such panic that she slipped on a small rug and broke her arm.

"But why did she run, Katish?" I inquired later that evening.

"Because she is wearing pink challis negligee," Katish replied.

"Good heavens! There's nothing peek-a-boo about that negligee," I protested.

"Is garment for boudoir," Katish answered gravely. "And, too, your Mother has kick off the shoes. They are under sofa, so no chance she get them on in time."

"It's the cat's pajamas," Bob mourned, shaking his head at me.

Katish was firmly convinced that Mother had taken the only course open to a lady. The fact that the insurance man had had to carry Mother up to bed, challis wrapper, bare feet, and all, was regrettable, but surely he could see that that couldn't be helped.

Katish had brought out the brandy bottle and carefully held a tiny glass to Mother's white lips. The salesman was visibly shaken, so Katish generously indicated the bottle and a tumbler to him. He poured out a good three fingers to steady himself. Then he stooped to pick up the policies and papers that he had dropped in the confusion. "Good God!" he exclaimed. "And I had this fine accident policy all ready for the signature." For a moment he looked hopeful again.

But Katish shook her head at him. "Is the right arm that is broken," she reminded.

"Yes, that's right," he agreed, crestfallen. "But I'll be back in a couple of weeks."

That was the only occasion on which I ever knew good liquor to be used for strictly medicinal purposes in our house!

Aunt Martha used to purse her lips and shake her head when she saw Bob and me enjoying delectable brandy-soaked Moscow Cherries. She thought some confection from the corner candy store much more suitable to our years.

I would sit patiently for hours sorting and cleaning big black Bing cherries for this wonderful treat—even though I knew full well that I should never be allowed to eat more than a tongue-teasing few. Mr. Roosevelt was well into his second term and Prohibition was no more, before I ever got enough of them. But, just once, Bob did manage to satisfy his appetite—in fact he overdid it, much to his regret! You'll understand his temptation after you've read the recipe.

MOSCOW CHERRIES

Select large, sweet, and perfect black cherries. Wipe each carefully with a cloth dipped in brandy, being careful not to break off the stem. Place the cherries loosely in sterile jars, stems up, and cover them with the following syrup: Cook together 3 cups of sugar and 1 cup of water and a ½ inch length of vanilla bean to form a fairly thick syrup. Cool slightly, remove the vanilla, and then mix in a good high proof brandy in the proportion of 1½ cups of brandy to 1 cup of syrup. Pour this over the cherries so that jars are filled to the top and seal.

This will be done in summer, of course, when cherries are ripe. Put the jars away until early December. Then take out the cherries and drain them well. Melt some bitter-sweet dipping chocolate over hot water. Dip the cherries one by one, making sure that each is thoroughly coated and that the chocolate forms a seal around the stem joint. Put them on waxed paper to harden and store them in tins, nesting them gently in strips of tissue paper. Serve at tea time or with the after-dinner coffee.

Use the delicious cherry brandy remaining in the jars for a superior topping for vanilla ice cream. It will keep indefinitely, and is a comfort to have on hand for those times when store ice cream has to be served in an emergency to guests who deserve better of you.

These cherries have none of the sweet insipidity of the candy store variety smothered in fondant. When Katish made them for us, cherries brandied and chocolate-coated with their stems on were a novelty. Today they can be bought in many shops, but they won't taste like Katish's.

It is one of my annual duties to prepare for Bob a box of brandied cherries in commemoration of the day when he criminally confiscated a big boxful intended for Aunt Martha. Bob had been intrusted with the precious cargo with instructions to deliver it promptly to her apartment as a surprise gift for a tea party that she was giving the next day. But on the way there, temptation overcame Bob. He pulled his rickety Menace to the side of the road, opened the fragrant box, and relaxed into bliss, spitting cherry stones dreamily in all directions. When he had consumed the very last pungent morsel, he drove to a candy store, and sacrificing his week's allowance, bought a flossy package of chocolates for Aunt Martha.

Of course he must have known that in time his guilty secret would come out. When Aunt Martha thanked Mother for a box of chocolate creams, the discrepancy was going to be painfully apparent. What he didn't know was that it was going to be extremely painfully apparent before the day was done.

For, half an hour before dinner time, Bob took to his bed with a violent stomachache. At first he tried to pretend that it was a headache, but nature didn't let him get away with this deception. Katish deserted her pots and pans to look after him, and Mother hurriedly called the doctor. Bob was sort of green and white, in stripes. It wasn't until the doctor muttered something about poison and the possible need for a stomach pump that Bob came through with his confession. Then he admitted that he had eaten nearly three pounds of brandied cherries on top of two hot dogs "with everything" and a pint of milk! I was awed by his daring and a little envious in spite of the result.

Mother decided to let her sister-in-law go on believing that she had been overcome by a sudden desire to present her with a very large and very pink box of questionable chocolate creams. Aunt Martha was already sufficiently impressed with her nephew's capacity for mischief.

A simple dessert that called on the family "medicine" cabinet for its final touch was winter pears with a fluffy sauce of sherry and eggs. Katish had a strange name for this sauce—hot water! I've never found out why it should be called this.

WINTER PEARS WITH SHERRY SAUCE

Bake peeled, cored winter pears in a covered dish in a medium oven, basting with heavy sugar syrup in which a 1 inch length of vanilla bean has been boiled. When pears are tender, chill thoroughly. Have the sherry sauce hot.

SHERRY SAUCE

Mix well in a small enamel saucepan ½ cup of sugar, 2 egg yolks, and 1 whole egg and a pinch of salt. Add slowly, stirring gently with a wooden spoon, ⅓ cup of dry sherry mixed with 3 tablespoons of cold water. Put the pan over a very low fire and cook, stirring constantly, until mixture coats the spoon. Put over hot water to keep warm, and just before serving, turn up the fire under the pan of hot water while you beat the sauce for a minute or two with a rotary beater. Serve immediately.

In gratitude for Katish's care of her often neglected infants, Julio's wife sent her a recipe for a cold, really fool-proof zabaione.

It is not so rich as the hot zabaione served in Italian restaurants, but for this very reason, we liked it better.

COLD ZABAIONE

Make a custard in the top of the double boiler set over hot water by stirring into ½ cup of sugar, 2 egg yolks, unbeaten, and a few grains of salt, then adding very gradually, stirring constantly, ½ cup of Marsala wine mixed with ¼ cup of water. (You can use sherry, if you prefer.) Stir this mixture constantly over the hot water until it begins to thicken. Then stir in ½ envelope of gelatin which has been softened in a little cold water. Take from fire. If the custard does not appear perfectly smooth, beat it up well with a rotary beater at this point. When cool and slightly thickened, add 2 stiffly beaten egg whites and a few drops of vanilla. Pour into glasses and chill.

Aunt Martha's activities among the Russian residents of Los Angeles had added a number of Russians to our list of friends. Many of these people were Katish's friends too. A large number of them, of any age from eighteen to fifty, were enrolled in American colleges, determined to start their lives in their new country under as little handicap as possible. Naturally, it meant a long, hard struggle for them to work their way through, and one of Katish's good meals was a definite bright spot in their lives. Mother had always kept open house on Sunday nights. We children were free to ask any of our friends to supper without notice. Seeing how much our Russian acquaintances enjoyed Katish's cooking and easy, informal hospitality, Mother began urging them to drop in on Sunday afternoon and stay to supper. Russians seem to be endowed with a natural social grace; and much more to the point, Bob and I thought at the time, a happy facility in languages and mathematics. Our friends were anxious to make any repayment they could and they never showed any impatience when Bob and I decoyed them into corners to beg their assistance with the French or mathematics we had neglected for a week.

Heartened by a plate of Katish's kidney stew which had benefited by some of Julio's red wine, they romped through our simple problems with positive pleasure. The kidney stew was always accompanied by flaky boiled rice and a great bowl of green salad. It was lavish hospitality at little cost.

KIDNEY STEW

Take 1 small young beef kidney or 8 lamb kidneys. Split them and remove the tubes. (Katish kept a pair of sharp, curved nail scissors for this, a useful tip that she had picked up, surprisingly enough, in casual conversation with a young and pretty Russian princess at a charity ball in Hollywood!) Wash the kidneys and cut into pieces. Squeeze out the water and put the kidneys into a bowl and cover them with dry red wine.

Let the kidneys stand in the wine for two or three hours. Then drain them well. Chop a large onion, brown it in bacon fat, and put it aside. Salt, pepper, and lightly flour the kidneys, and sauté them quickly in hot bacon fat. Dust with 2 scant tablespoons of flour and stir briskly until the flour is absorbed in the fat. Then stir in ½ cup of red wine. Let cook down a little, then add 1½ cups of water, a little brown meat essence, and finally, ½ cup of sour cream. Simmer for about five minutes. Just before serving, sprinkle a finely chopped, hard-cooked egg and a spoonful of dill or parsley over the top of the stew.

Though Katish was always concerned for the lonely, neglected existence of the bachelors among her acquaintances and ours, and would spend hours preparing some favorite dish for one of them, she showed no inclination to respond to romantic advances. It was seldom that she so much as consented to accompany any man to the movies. She had known one happy marriage, ended with the death of her young husband in the war, and she seemed to feel no desire to marry again. We were selfishly pleased by her attitude. That her heart was not without its due share of romance, however, was amply proved by her feat in sitting three times through the picture *Seventh Heaven*. Katish found in the movies a never-failing source of charm and amusement. She chose the sentimental offerings which Bob particularly scorned. After one or two of the rootin', tootin', shootin' kind that he favored, she flatly refused to accompany him. Fond as we were of Katish, we didn't much regret the loss of her company, for she repeatedly embarrassed us by exclaiming aloud at tense moments in the picture.

"Ai! ai! ohoo!" she would breathe in mounting suspense and terror as our hero went slipping and sliding down some steep and treacherous hillside on his trusty horse. "Ahhhh. *Slava Bogu*," she would sigh ("Glory to God"), as he reached level ground, every hair of his head handsomely in place.

"Now remember, Katish, we aren't in church," Bob said to her once as he turned from the ticket booth and escorted us into the theatre. "You'll have to behave yourself."

This strange admonition grew out of our recent visit to the Russian Church with Katish. Bob had been impressed by the fact that the worshipers had entered and left the church at will with no apparent regard for a beginning or end to the services. This causes less commotion than one might suppose, though, for the congregation stands or kneels, but there are no pews; it is never necessary to push one's way past long legs or plump knees to get into a seat. Newcomers softly greet friends, and sometimes whispered conversations are held without drawing any frowns. All this seemed delightfully informal to us, used as we were to hurrying to be on time, and then sitting in enforced rigid inattention through the services of our own church. So Bob cautioned Katish, when she attended the movies, not to behave as if she were in church!

Mother seemed to feel that two children, a host of friends, and a fair quota of solicitous relatives were enough to fill up her life after Father's death. One or two faithful old beaux came regularly to our Sunday suppers, but I don't think it ever entered Mother's head that she might actually marry one of them. Now and then Bob and I would begin to fear that we might find ourselves with a step-father and we would glower spitefully at any man of suitable age who came often to the house. But our fears were soon dispelled by Mother's cheerful, open friendliness toward the unfortunate suspect.

With Aunt Martha it was different. So far as any of us knew, only one man had ever shown any desire to win her heart. And he had mysteriously disappeared a week before their scheduled wedding. It was believed that he had been accidentally drowned while canoeing, but it was never proved, as his body was not found. Bob and I privately thought that he'd simply come to his senses and skipped in the nick of time. Aunt Martha was too frankly bossy, we thought, ever to attract a husband. But masculine attention caused her to bridle and exhibit an old-fashioned coyness.

"Poor Martha wouldn't be so bossy if she had someone to look after," Mother said tolerantly.

We all opened our eyes and perked up our ears when Aunt Martha began to appear repeatedly on Sunday nights accompanied by a rotund Russian gentleman with the delightful name of Nicolai Andreyevich Krasnoperov—Nicholas Andrey Redfeather, in translation. He was a lighthearted little man, fond of good food and drink and a merry song. After he began to feel at home with us he even brought along a balalaika and played and sang gay Russian songs for us. He was a wonderful addition to our parties and we wondered if a snare of matrimony cast by Aunt Martha would make him a permanent part of our lives. We rather hoped so, for we felt that he would make a jolly uncle.

Mr. Krasnoperov, a gentleman of considerable intellectual attainments, we were given to understand by our aunt, had been forced by the rude exigencies of exile to take up the trade of house painting. In Russia, he had never done anything except have a wonderful time with the money his ancestors had accumulated. Unfortunately, English was not among his attainments; and, judging by his happy disregard for the handicap, it never would be. Twice a week, in the evening, he visited Aunt Martha for an hour's lesson in English. But either she was a poor teacher, or little Mr. Redfeather was an inattentive pupil, for his difficulties with the language seemed to increase rather than lessen as time went on.

His gaiety and abundant good will sufficed for social purposes, but in business he seemed doomed to failure, until our determined and resourceful aunt took matters in hand. To her agile intellect the jump from house painter to interior decorator was a trifling one. Within a month after the idea had got hold of Aunt Martha, Mr. Krasnoperov was established in a smart little decorator's shop in Beverly Hills. The fact that the man's notions of interior decoration were bound to be somewhat unorthodox would make little difference there—it might even carry him to untold heights of success. As a matter of record, her protégé did exhibit an unsuspected talent for the artistic side of his new profession, adamantly refusing to supply his clients with the rust or flame-red velveteen draperies and the wrought-iron fireside benches that all their neighbors were frenziedly purchasing for their haciendas in Hollywood, thereby bewildering and impressing them no end. Aunt Martha would buzz out once or twice a week in her electric to look after the financial end of the business. We had to chalk up a good deed for our bossy relative, for a bit of bossing seemed to be just what Mr. Redfeather needed.

"There is just one thing lacking to make the venture a roaring success," she remarked pensively, one evening. "Now, Mr. Krasnoperov, if you only had a title, people would flock to you to have their houses done. Of course, I'm anything but a snob, I will say for myself, but I quite see that it gives a certain something to be able to say that Prince So-and-So has just done one's house. No-ooo—I don't think the title of prince is so good any more. There do seem to be so many of them. But baron, perhaps Mr. Krasnoperov, are you sure there isn't a title in your family that you would have the right to use? It would be a help."

Mr. K. swallowed audibly. We all turned to him and were amazed to see that the little man had turned white. "My kind friend," he stammered, "I to beg say *niet*—no! *Niet, niet, pajaloosta!* Please!" He ended in what was practically a moan.

Aunt Martha had finally to give up the idea. Mr. Krasnoperov was adamant if not eloquent. We speculated on his possible feelings and reasons. Of course, we could see that he wasn't the sort of person to use a title that did not belong to him, but we didn't see why the mere suggestion should cause him such acute distress. He was so evidently disturbed by the conversation that Mother sent Bob for the brandy bottle. After a couple of pegs with soda he was his old gay self playing his balalaika and caroling *Bublitchki*.

Nicolai
Andreyevich
Krasnoperov
playing his balalaika

Excitement was rampant among us when a few days later Aunt Martha came over and asked Katish to teach her to make rum babas. We knew that the newly made interior decorator was inordinately fond of this rich dessert, and we also knew that Aunt Martha never did any cooking if she could help it. She would set a man up in business and think little of it; but when she showed herself willing to learn to cook for him, we suspected that nothing less than love could motivate the sacrifice. Katish and Aunt Martha shut themselves in the kitchen for most of the day, and when it was over, Bob and I tried to pump Katish for any information she might have gathered.

But, "Your aunt is very good, kind woman. That all I know," was as much as we could get out of our dear Katish.

RUM BABA

Scald ½ cup of milk. Cool the milk to lukewarm and dissolve in it 1 cake of fresh yeast. In another bowl beat 2 egg yolks until thick and gradually add ¾ cup of sugar. Add 1 whole egg, beating vigorously. Melt ¼ cup of sweet butter and add while slightly warm to the egg mixture. Add ½ vanilla bean, finely cut. Stir in the milk and yeast mixture and then beat in enough sifted flour—about 1¼ cups—to make a medium thick batter. Let rise three and a half hours in a warm place.

Butter a large ring mold or individual baking cups and fill barely half full. Let the batter rise again, and bake at 350° until a straw comes out clean. Take from pans and cool on rack.

Prepare a syrup of ½ cup of sugar and ¾ cup of apricot juice boiled together for ten minutes. Add 1 teaspoon of lemon juice and a generous jigger of medium dark rum and pour carefully over cake. Put the cake back into the mold to marinate for several hours. Just before serving, pour some additional rum over the cake. Fill the center of the cake ring with ice cream sauce and pile pitted black cherries over the top.

ICE CREAM SAUCE

Allow a pint of vanilla ice cream to soften slightly. Then mix in 1 beaten egg and 2 tablespoons of rum. Beat together well and put into refrigerator trays to harden and keep until ready to use. This sauce is good for many desserts.

We seldom had rum-flavored desserts back in the Prohibition years. I don't know whether rum was particularly difficult to obtain, or if Mother just felt that a lady couldn't very well present a prescription for grog. At any rate, a few cherished bottles were made to last for several years. Another dessert which called for some of that precious supply, but seemed well worth the sacrifice, was peaches in rum.

PEACHES IN RUM

Slice juicy, fragrant ripe peaches into a serving bowl. For about 3 cups of the fruit, mix together half a cup of good honey and a jigger of rum. Pour this libation over the fruit and chill thoroughly before serving. If you wish, you can pour an extra dollop of rum into the bowl just before it reaches the table and set it alight. Ladle the burning liquor over the ice-cold fruit and enjoy the contented faces of your guests along with your own good food.

We were never fond of whipped cream. Fresh fruits were always served with a pitcher of rich liquid cream or marinated in a liquor that blended well with the particular fruit. Toward the end of the strawberry season, when we had all grown a little indifferent to strawberries and cream, Katish would bring out the port bottle and give us the luscious red berries made exciting with the addition of a little of the ruby wine.

STRAWBERRIES IN PORT

Wash and hull your berries as usual; drain them very well and put into a glass serving bowl. Sprinkle sugar to taste over the fruit and then pour over a glass of port wine. Cover closely and put into the refrigerator to chill for an hour. Do not let the berries stand too long as they soften rapidly under this treatment.

CHAPTER FOUR

Katish was not only the best cook we had ever had, she was by far the most orderly and efficient. Since her incumbency in our kitchen was as much a friendly arrangement as a financial one, she was free to do as she liked with a good deal of her time.

In the afternoons she often elected to help Mother in the garden, unless it was Julio's day to come for the heavy digging and pruning. Then she kept to her pots and pans or went out visiting or to the movies. She knew all too well that Julio would somehow succeed in annoying her so that he could dance maddeningly around her, licking his dirty old finger and pretending that she gave off a Pssst! like a hot iron when he touched her. Probably the trick would have lost its pleasure for the old rogue if she could just once have managed to ignore his foolishness. But for all her kindness, Katish had a bit of a temper. When she heard Americans use the expression, "a bit of a Tartar," she was amused and interested. "*Da*, yes, I am bit of Tartar," she said, meaning it literally. One of her grandmothers had been a pretty Tartar girl whom her grandfather had married while stationed on military duty in the Crimea.

Katish had no set day off, but some time off nearly every day and, at least once a week, Mother would insist that she do no housework or cooking, even if she chose to spend the day at home. When she found that Mother really worried about taking advantage of her willingness, Katish gave in and took her day off. But she always made the house shiningly clean on the preceding day, and when Mother went out to the kitchen, she usually found some favorite casserole dish prepared and awaiting reheating for our dinner.

Sometimes there was an earthen casserole of golubtsy, ready to be put into the oven for a half-hour and then served as a one-dish meal with fragrant slices of dark pumpernickel and sweet butter, and some of the crispy, half-pickled cucumbers that are to be found in Russian delicatessen stores as *molosolni agurchiki*. Golubtsy is a Russian dish that has a counterpart in most of the nations of Europe.

GOLUBTSY

Cook ½ cup of rice in a little less than a cup of boiling, salted water until it is almost soft enough for regular use. Let it cool. Chop 1 medium onion fine and then mix the onion, rice, and 1 pound of coarsely ground raw beef. Season the mixture well with salt and pepper. Remove whole leaves from a well-shaped cabbage and scald them. Sprinkle the leaves with salt and pepper and put a large spoonful of the rice and meat filling in the center of each. Roll up and tie or skewer with picks. Heat some bacon fat in a heavy pan or earthen casserole and carefully, lightly, brown the cabbage bundles. Remove the bundles from the pan and stir a tablespoon of flour into the drippings; add 1½ cups of tomato purée and juice. Season to taste and add a bay leaf and stir in ¾ cup of sour cream. Put the cabbage rolls back into the pan, cover, and cook in a moderate oven for an hour.

When Katish came in from an afternoon spent with friends or window shopping in the city, she was voluble about her experiences. There was never any mystery as to how she spent these daylight hours. But very often she went out at eight o'clock or thereabouts, when dinner was over and the dishes neatly put away, and returned in the small hours of the morning. At breakfast she was invariably bright-eyed and, except for rare occasions, wonderfully cheerful. Mother wouldn't discuss the matter with me, but I knew that she wondered where Katish had been, and whether it was mere coincidence that kept her from giving an account of such evenings. Mother wasn't actually worried—just full of good old-fashioned feminine curiosity. But it wasn't any of her business and, much as she wanted to know, she couldn't bring herself to ask what our cook did during these long night hours away from home.

Of course it had to be on a night when Aunt Martha was visiting us that we found out. Mother had asked Katish if she wouldn't like to have a little evening party occasionally for her friends. She could use the dining room which was across the wide hall from the living room and quite large and comfortable. There were two or three easy chairs and a sofa, and the dining table could be folded and placed against the wall, making a second living room that we children often used when we had our young friends in.

Katish had never availed herself of the privilege until that night, when for some reason or other, Aunt Martha was staying with us. Mother was pleased when Katish said that she would like to use the dining room after dinner. She told her to go ahead and prepare some nice refreshments for her guests, to take the phonograph into the dining room, and to be sure and have a good time. Katish thanked her and said that she would prepare some refreshments, but they wouldn't want the phonograph.

After dinner, Mother, Aunt Martha, Bob, and I went into the living room to spend an evening in reading and desultory family conversation. We questioned our aunt about Mr. Krasnoperov's latest decorating commissions, watching her closely for signs of tell-tale confusion at the mention of her newest protégé's name, but we didn't learn a thing, except that he was doing as well as could be expected. (Rather better, we thought, since he was earning a fair living at a profession adopted on a moment's notice, at our aunt's inspiration.) We gave up the useless probing.

At about ten o'clock Mother remarked, "I wonder if Katish and her friends decided to go out. There isn't a sound from the dining room."

"I've noticed that, too," Aunt Martha said. "I heard them come in at about eight-thirty, but there's been hardly a sound since. I'm sure we'd have heard them if they'd all gone out together. Now what do you suppose they can be up to in there?"

Bob and I pricked up our ears. We didn't want to give Aunt Martha any encouragement, but come to think of it, we were curious too.

"Of course Katish is a priest's daughter," Aunt Martha remarked once reassuringly, as if to herself. Mother just looked at her and I was glad I wasn't Aunt Martha. We all went back to our reading, but it wasn't ten minutes before our persistent relative was at it again. "I simply must have a drink of water," she announced suddenly.

Mother quickly asked Bob to go upstairs and get a glass of water from the bathroom. You couldn't get to the kitchen without going through the dining room. But Aunt Martha meant to get that glass of water herself, and she was going to get it from the kitchen. Mother sighed and gave it up. Our aunt got up and marched across the hall. We heard her tap on the sliding doors and then fling them wide, as if about to expose scenes of high orgy. The silence continued. In a moment Aunt Martha was back.

"You should just see what's going on in there!" she exploded. "And WHO is in there. Priest's daughter indeed!"

The doors to the dining room were still open and Mother looked uneasy. "Go and shut the doors," she instructed Bob.

"Do you mean to say that you don't care what goes on under your own roof?" Aunt Martha demanded in shocked tones.

Mother got up and went to close the doors herself. I tagged along, decency thrown to the winds by this time. The scene in the dining room was interesting; I'm glad I didn't miss it. Around the table five people were sitting. The most arresting of these was a monumental red-faced gentleman in the neat blue of the city police force. He was tilted precariously on the back legs of his chair and gazing at the ceiling with a rapt air. On either side of him there slouched a seedy individual in clothes that looked as if they had been regularly slept in. Both of these far-from-natty gentlemen appeared to be in need of a square meal.

There was a large woman with very yellow hair, but a well-scrubbed look and tidy black clothing; and there was Katish, large as life and twice as natural. She spread out on the table the five cards she held and then looked up and smiled cheerfully at Mother. The policeman's chair came down to rest on four legs with a bang and the smug look left his face. Katish had reason to be cheerful—five good reasons that added up to a royal flush!

Mother went back to the living room and Bob and I trotted at her heels. This looked like an interesting night at our house.

"Poker! Those people are actually playing poker in there without so much as a by-your-leave!" Aunt Martha choked as we came in.

"Why, Martha, is that what it is? I'm afraid I don't recognize many card games, since I don't care for anything but bridge myself," Mother confessed. "But they do seem to be enjoying themselves."

"Well," Aunt Martha sniffed, "you and I never did agree about things like that." She changed her attack. "But what do you think of her guests? How do you know we won't all be murdered in our beds with people like that brought right into the house?"

Mother looked a little concerned. "I didn't especially like the looks of those two men. But the policeman is reassuring. I'm certain it will be all right, Martha."

"Where do you suppose she found such people?" Aunt Martha puzzled. "They look like the sort you see leaning against the alley fence, down and out and asking for dimes."

"Oh, that's easy," Bob told her airily. "You see, they probably wanted a couple of hands for the game, so the policeman yanked these two out of the Black Maria. He'll put 'em back and haul 'em in when they've finished the game. If you look out front, you'll see the wagon parked there, sure."

Aunt Martha started out of her chair as he spoke, then sank back and stared indignantly at him.

"Go to bed, Sis and Bob," Mother ordered in the voice that meant, "And no dallying." Reluctantly, we went.

We learned the next morning that the party had been a success. The two unprepossessing gentlemen probably were bums, Katish conceded. The players she had expected hadn't been able to come, so her friend, the policeman, had found these two at the last moment. What a pity that Aunt Martha hadn't looked out for the wagon the night before. It might have been there, scandalously parked at our respectable door!

The blond lady was a Swedish masseuse, a very nice woman, and her hair was just naturally that color. She, Katish, and the policeman, together with a number of other "nice, quiet people," frequently played poker, sometimes at the apartment of the masseuse, sometimes at other homes. Katish loved it, and usually she won.

No wonder she was so cheerful at breakfast after her nights out!

Katish had made a great platter of small beef piroshkee—meat pies—for her guests. And she had made generous sandwiches of a delectable liver spread. They had had red salmon egg caviar and little green onions on rye bread, too. And near-beer and coffee and a rum pie. The two seedy guests must have felt that it was a good address to remember. Mother worried about that until Katish remarked that she wouldn't have them again, not for anything! They were terrible poker players.

In some cities the red salmon eggs that Katish served are obtainable in bulk, only lightly salted. They are very good this way, and inexpensive. Pile them on crisp French bread or black pumpernickel and sprinkle with finely chopped green onion. San Francisco, Los Angeles, and Seattle, all within quick shipping distance of houses handling the Columbia River salmon, have little Russian grocery stores where fresh red caviar can be bought. And marvelous smoked salmon, rich and smooth as butter, subtly smoky, but innocent of salt, and the crisp Russian pickles can be found in these dark little shops!

The liver paste is wonderful for hearty sandwiches or for cocktail canapés. It's a spread that men particularly like. Katish usually made up enough for several days and kept it in a closed jar in the refrigerator.

LIVER SPREAD

Ask your butcher for ½ pound of tender young beef or lamb liver. In your heavy frying pan, heat 1 tablespoon of bacon fat. In it, brown a small onion, sliced thinly. Flour the sliced liver and sauté it to a nice brown in more of the drippings. Let it cool and then put it, along with the onion slices and 1 small green onion or 1 tablespoon of chives, and the tiniest possible sliver of garlic, through the medium knife of the food chopper. Then put the mixture through the fine knife, twice.

Put the paste into a bowl and add the bacon drippings you used for browning the onion and liver. Mix it in well. Add softened butter or cream until the mixture is of a good spreading consistency. Salt it well and grind in a zesty amount of fresh black pepper; don't let this spread be flat! Stir and mash with a fork until it is all satin-smooth and perfectly blended. Put in a tightly capped jar and store in the refrigerator. It improves with a day's ripening.

BEEF PIROSHKEE

Brown a pound of good quality ground beef in butter or other fat. Cool. Add 1 large onion, chopped and sautéed to a golden brown. Chop two hard-boiled eggs and mix in lightly. Season the mixture well with salt and pepper. Stir 1 teaspoon of flour into the drippings left from browning meat and onion. Add ½ cup of water and salt and pepper to make a thin, very brown gravy. Pour this over the meat and let it cool thoroughly. Put small mounds of this filling on rounds of puff pastry, seal the edges with milk, and bake in a 450° oven.

KATISH'S EASY PUFF PASTRY

Cut ¼ pound of sweet butter into 2 cups of all-purpose flour, leaving the mixture in coarse lumps. (Puff pastry is not usually salted, but Katish added 1½ teaspoons of salt to the flour when making piroshkee.) Then stir in the smallest possible amount of cold sour cream that will bind the mixture together. Do not use any water at all. Be sure that the butter is cool and firm and the sour cream very cold when you start to work.

Gather the dough into a ball and roll it out on a floured board. Take 2 tablespoons of cold butter and cut it into very small bits.

Scatter the bits over the rolled-out dough and fold it into three thicknesses. Roll out again, fold in three, press down, and wrap the dough in waxed paper. Store in the refrigerator for two hours or longer, until ready to bake. Roll the pastry just once this time, to the desired thickness, and use immediately. Bake in a 450° oven.

RUM OR BRANDY PIE

Prepare a baked pie shell of flaky pastry or use your own favorite crumb pastry to line a glass serving dish. Then beat the yolks of 4 eggs until light, add ⅞ cup of sugar. Soak 1 tablespoon of gelatin in ½ cup of cold water. Put the gelatin and water over a low fire and let it come to a boil, then pour it over the sugar and egg mixture, stirring briskly. Whip 1 pint of cream stiff (using a commercial whipping preparation if necessary); add 1 teaspoon vanilla. Fold the cream into the egg mixture, and flavor with 2 tablespoons of brandy or rum. Cool, but do not allow to set, and pour into the pastry or crumb shell. When the filling is set, sprinkle the top of the pie heavily with shaved bitter-sweet chocolate curls and finely chopped pistachio nuts. Or decorate the top with perfect strawberries which have stood for a time in a little of the liquor and sugar to sweeten.

Mother was a very good cook, but so long as a competent cook presided in the kitchen she felt no unconquerable urge to concern herself in the preparation of meals. She did ask Katish to teach me something about cooking, when she wasn't too busy, and with the strict understanding that I should wash my own dishes and clean up any mess I made. On those hard terms my interest was pretty much limited to cakes and candies for personal consumption. But then Katish, kind-hearted as always, reasoned that if I prepared some dish for dinner that she would have had to make herself otherwise, it was only fair that she should wash the used cups and bowls and mixing spoons that strewed my path. The logic of this was easily apparent to me, so I did do quite a bit of cooking under her supervision.

If school friends were coming in for the evening, I would devote my skill to the preparation of sweets. One that we liked and which Mother approved as being good-for-us as well as good, was Katish's fruit roll.

FRUIT ROLL

Put 2 cups of white sugar and ½ cup of milk over a low fire and cook, stirring constantly, for ten minutes. Add 1½ cups of dried apricots which have been steamed until tender and cut in strips. Or use prunes, tenderized and coarsely chopped. Cook and stir the mixture until it begins to leave the sides of the pan. Add 3 tablespoons of butter and cook to the soft ball stage. Take from fire, let cool two minutes and then beat until stiff, adding 1 teaspoon of vanilla and 1 cup of broken walnut meats. When too stiff to beat, pour onto a damp towel and roll up in the towel to cool and harden. Slice in thin rounds.

While I worked I was apt to pester Katish for stories of her life in Russia. She liked to talk of the past. If I had been confined to the house for bad behavior I found it a comfort to extract from her some story that proved grown-ups hadn't been born with all their saint-like qualities in full bloom. It was easy to guess that Katish had been a spirited girl, and she told me an amusing tale from the days of her husband's courtship.

Katish was seventeen when relatives invited her to come for a winter to their home in the capital city of their province. They wanted to give their poor little country cousin a season of gaiety, and perhaps a chance to make a good match. Katish promptly upset the applecart by falling in love with a distant cousin whom she met for the first time in her relatives' house. The young man was an officer of the Imperial Army but unfortunately he possessed no private fortune. This was a grave lack in the eyes of Katish's prosperous relatives. In vain did Katish and Alex protest that they could live happily on his modest military pay. The match was frowned upon and the man made to feel that he had overstepped the bounds of propriety and hospitality in winning the heart of Katish.

Alex had a sister, Tania, who became very fond of Katish and eagerly played the role of go-between for her brother and his sweetheart. But notes and messages relayed by another only sharpened their desire to be alone together. Alex felt that he could no longer visit Katish at her uncle's house. So she was delighted when she was asked to a large ball where all the officers garrisoned in the town would be present. Her elderly uncle would escort her to the party; his wife's health did not permit her attendance. But for days Katish and the good lady discussed the gown that Katish would wear on the important night. Katish longed to wear a lovely sea-green evening dress that had been ordered for her from Moscow. Her severe aunt thought that she should appear in the bouffant white which best becomes a young girl. The elderly relative had her way; Katish could not protest too loudly when it was only through her aunt's kindness that she had the choice of two such lovely gowns.

On the night of the ball Katish and her dignified escort set forth with Katish looking demure in white. Hardly had they paid their respects to their hostess when Alex came to claim Katish. For a time they waltzed happily. Then Alex suggested a daring plan. He would call an *izvoschik* to take them for a sleigh ride. The elderly uncle had long since disappeared into the card room. Katish knew that it would be a shocking thing for a girl to leave a party alone with a young man—but that was just what made it irresistible, the chance to be alone for once with the man she was determined to marry.

Alex slipped away and came back to signal that the sleigh was waiting at the side door; he had found Katish's cape for her and Tania was keeping an eye out to see that they were not observed. She would make some excuse for Katish if anyone inquired. Wrapped in a rough fur robe the lovers drove contentedly through the deserted streets; everyone of consequence was at the ball, and the little provincial capital boasted no brilliant street lights to disclose their identity should anyone of their acquaintance be abroad.

For a long time they let the old *izvoschik* drive where his fancy dictated. But suddenly Alex thought to look at his watch. He cried out to the driver to turn back immediately; they must fly if Katish

was to be back at the ball in time to say goodnight to her hostess and make her demure departure on the arm of her uncle.

There was a lovely sensation of flying over the hard-packed snow; laughing with sheer enjoyment they slipped low in the seat of the sleigh to avoid the occasional clods of snow that the horse's hoofs threw backward with stinging force. At a dark corner their driver tried to slow up to make the turn. But just then another sleigh hurtled out of the blackness with a speed and suddenness that frightened their horse. He bolted on the narrow turn, and over went their sleigh, tipping Katish, Alex, and the driver in a helpless tangle on the dirty, heaped-up snow at the side of the road! For a moment the two youngsters were overcome by irrepressible merriment. Rocking with giggles, they assured each other that they were unhurt and struggled to their feet. But then Katish remembered her fragile white gown. Even in the dark she knew that it must be hopelessly stained and perhaps torn. How could she go back to the ball now, even if there were time?

The other sleigh had pulled up a little way down the street. Now the driver turned around and came up to them to see if he could be of assistance. With thanksgiving, Alex recognized a brother officer driving his own notably fast horses. Tossing some money to their alternately praying and cursing *izvoschik*, Alex helped Katish into his friend's sleigh. "Go like the wind, Dmitri Antonovich, for the love of God!" he implored. "We must get back to Madame Altinov's ball before the dancing ends."

Dmitri Antonovich didn't need to be told how serious it would be if such an escapade were discovered. Not even the shreds of a girl's reputation would have been left for scandal to play with in a Russian provincial town if it became known that she had run off unchaperoned from a party.

But now Katish's wits had returned. She directed the young officer to take them first to her uncle's house; to wait quietly at the yard gates. With the speed of desperation she darted into the sleeping house. The servant who nodded inside the hall, waiting up for the young lady and the master, never heard her light, flying steps.

Short minutes later, Katish sped back through the gates. Pulling aside the dark wrap she wore, she showed the young men a lovely sea-green gown. "My kind old uncle is so absent-minded, perhaps he will not notice that this is not the gown I wore to the ball, and the others hardly saw me before we left," she explained breathlessly as they tore through the deserted, icy streets, back to the music and lights and dancing.

Katish and Alex had the last half of a waltz before her uncle came to take her to say goodnight to her hostess. With a rapidly beating heart Katish approached the august lady. Even if he suspected something amiss, her uncle could be trusted to say nothing here. But what of the others?

"My dear child, I do hope you haven't been hiding in the cloak room," the hostess said to Katish. "I've hardly seen that pretty green gown about the floor. Do forgive me if I forgot to look after you properly and see that you were introduced."

Young Tania, Alex's sister, stood by regarding her future sister-in-law with a look that mingled puzzlement for the green gown and congratulations for something put over on the grown-ups. Katish blushed rosily as she assured the kind lady that she had had the most wonderful evening of her life. She would never forget it! Trying to look calm and self-confident, she took her uncle's thin old arm and went with him to that side door where sleighs were now being brought for their owners. The old man yawned sleepily. "How pretty you look, my dear!" he said. "But I could have sworn that you'd worn a white gown! Well, well, it just goes to show that I'm getting too old for this sort of thing. Absent-minded, as your aunt so often tells me."

Katish's nimble fingers and the thrifty lessons she had learned in her own home stood her in good stead that night. Before she went to sleep she had cleaned and mended the white gown so beautifully that only the closest inspection would reveal it had ever been damaged. Her aunt would rely on her for an account of the party, for her husband would never be able to recount what the women had worn or how the younger generation had behaved itself. Katish had little need to fear that her secret would come out now.

At her wedding to Alex, a year later, he and his best man, Dmitri

Antonovich, and laughing-eyed young Tania, drank a toast to the wit and daring of the bride. They drank alone and adamantly refused to explain their toast to anyone. But Katish's black eyes must have danced merrily and her round cheeks grown pink in remembrance, even as they did so many years later, when she related the story for the pleasure of a little American who was no stranger to mischief, but had never known the thrilling joy of a stolen sleigh ride.

CHAPTER FIVE

When Katish came to preside in our kitchen we were the complacent owners of just one set of old Haviland soup plates. They were the wide, flat, old-fashioned kind, with faded pink flowers on their rims, and just one stray blossom trailing to the bottom of the dish. They were very old and years of enthusiastic scraping had left that posy in the bottom very dim indeed. When Bob and I were small, we were always told that we must empty our plates until that little pink blossom emerged. After our Russian cook had been with us a few months, we had no less than four sets of soup bowls. Borsch, rich and red and glowing, was served in transparent old white Lenox plates that Katish had picked up in some antique shop.

"Katish is truly an artist," Mother praised. "I'm not sure it's right to hide her away in our kitchen."

Bob and I protested that she liked being in our kitchen, and besides, we liked having her there.

For thick soups Katish had bought some fat little gray crackleware bowls from Denmark. She had found them at the end of a long, tiring day of shopping at the huge and well-known store belonging to the M. family. The little bowls were so endearingly chubby, softly grayed, and pleasant to hold in the hand, that Katish could not resist carrying them directly home to show to Mother, although she already had accumulated a goodly number of bulky parcels in her day's trek through the stores. But, "*Da*, yes, I take," Katish told the clerk, and set off with the package tucked under her arm.

As she was leaving the store she remembered that she must go to the branch post office in the basement to buy stamps. Unfortunately, a lot of other people had had the same idea at the same time. Resignedly, Katish took her place at the end of the line. Of course the little man who is always there, well to the fore in any queue— the one who can't remember whether his cousin lives in Kamchatka or Kalamazoo, and what is the postage, please?—was there. Katish gave her attention to her parcels, rearranging them so that none should be lost. At last she was aware that the queue was moving and stepped forward. She almost trod on a short, very round little man. Most certainly, she remembered, he hadn't been in front of her a moment before. Her usual good nature worn thin by her tiring day, she determined not to put up with any nonsense.

"You mistake," she informed the interloper. Having no free hand she nudged him with the bulky package of soup bowls, which was squeezed tightly under her arm.

The man only shrugged; he didn't even turn around. This was too much. Katish stepped out of line; using a firm elbow, she placed herself ahead of him, where she belonged. The little man didn't like this and he began to argue vehemently. But Katish knew she was in the right and she quietly held her ground in spite of the fact that the man's protesting roars grew so violent that passing customers stopped to watch the fray. At length a portly, flustered gentleman stepped up and addressed himself to Katish.

"Just what seems to be the trouble, madam?" the newcomer inquired anxiously.

"It does not *seem*," Katish retorted. "And to please mind your own business, young man." She addressed any male, regardless of age, as "young man" when she wanted to put him in his place.

The fiftyish "young man" wrung his hands. "But my dear lady," he wailed, "I am trying to mind my own business. I am Mr. M."

"I do not see—" Katish began icily. Light dawned. It was Mr. M.'s

Katish demands her rights!

business indeed; he owned the store! "Then you must know that your customers do not care for this," she told Mr. M. sternly, indicating the fat man who was gibbering and shoving and yelping in thwarted rage.

Mr. M. was equal to the occasion. "If you will come with me, madam, I will see that you receive the stamps you want from my office," he offered gallantly. "Allow me to apologize for this unfortunate occurrence," he went on, glaring at the rude little man.

Katish graciously permitted Mr. M. to carry her parcels as far as his office, where stamps of all denominations were displayed for her choice with as much politeness and ceremony as if she were inspecting sables. From the comfortable chair she contracted for twenty three's and fifteen two's. After that, Katish and Mr. M. exchanged dignified bows when they met in the aisles of the store.

We enjoyed the lovely little crackle-ware bowls all the more for Katish's animated account of her adventure. They were just right for delicate green cream of asparagus soup with thin strips of pink ham to lend piquancy to taste and color.

Mother had an old ironstone soup tureen and a heavy silver ladle that had been put away for years. When Katish came across them, she insisted that soups must always be served from the tureen at the table. The tureen was not elegant, but it had somewhat the shape, and all the homely cosiness, of a fat setting hen. I still think soup tastes best when it is served from that tureen!

Most Russian soups, and the best ones, are made with a rich beef stock as the base. There is a belief among Americans that soup always tastes better the second day. This is simply because so few people take the trouble to prepare their base properly in the first place. And it really isn't much trouble. You can turn the fire low and forget about the stock pot for hours and hours. In fact, that is the best thing you can do.

Katish was particularly firm about selecting the bones for the stock pot. She insisted upon a fine large knuckle bone, cracked through. There had to be a shin bone with its small quantity of surrounding beef. And there were invariably the biggest marrow bones

Katish could persuade from the butcher. The bones and meat were wiped clean with a damp cloth and put into a large, heavy aluminum pot with a close-fitting cover. One or two carrots that had grown too large to suit Katish's notions of what a proper carrot should be were washed with a stiff brush and sliced thinly lengthwise. The carrots, an outer stick, and a few leaves of celery, two slices of potato, and a whole onion were dropped into the pot with the bones. The pot was filled with water, covered, and set to simmer gently.

Twice during the first hour, Katish skimmed the stock. And about half an hour after the water came to the simmering point, she took out the marrow bones, scraped out all the precious marrow, and put the bones back into the pot. Then, with the fire turned low, Katish forgot all about the stock pot while she went about her other work. It always simmered for at least four hours. If we were having boiled beef with the soup, Katish added it just in time to cook tender.

When the stock had simmered long enough, Katish strained the liquid into a smaller pot. Bones and limp vegetables were discarded. The stock was allowed to cool, and the congealed fat lifted easily from the top. Vegetables ("wegetables," Katish called them) were cut fairly small and put into a heavy pan with a good chunk of butter. They were put over a low fire to sweat for five minutes. Meantime the covered pan was vigorously shaken to prevent the vegetables from browning or sticking. This treatment gives the soup a fine, full-bodied flavor. Some of the beef fat taken from the pot can be used in place of butter if desired.

Our favorite Russian soup was borsch. My second choice was rasolnik, an unusual but delicious soup. Both are properly served with a spoonful of sour cream in each plate. Katish brought the sour cream to the table in a deep blue bowl, and we ladled it generously into our soup with a lovely old Russian silver spoon with a twisted handle.

And Katish saw to it that soup plates and tureen were warmed, so that soup was never less than piping hot in our house. It is astonishing that cold soup plates are so often found in houses where a cold dinner plate would not be tolerated.

BORSCH

Take two quarts of good beef stock. Melt 3 tablespoons of butter or beef fat in a heavy pan that can be well covered. Have ready 1 cup of finely chopped cabbage, 1 cup of diced potatoes, ½ cup of diced carrots, 1 stick minced celery, 1 small onion chopped. Put the vegetables into the fat, turn the fire low and shake the covered pan over the heat for about five minutes. Then add the vegetables to the hot stock.

Put 1½ cups of canned tomatoes through a sieve and into the stock. Add ½ cup of juice from a small can of beets. When the other vegetables are tender, add 1 cup of diced cooked or canned beets and 1 scant teaspoon of vinegar. Season well and turn off the fire before the beets lose their color. A dash of finely chopped dill or parsley should be sprinkled over the top of the soup after it has been transferred to the tureen. Borsch is one soup that quite definitely calls for the spoonful of sour cream in each serving.

RASOLNIK

To 2 quarts of beef stock add 1 large, coarsely cubed potato, ½ cup of finely cut carrot, and a bay leaf. When it has cooked for about ten minutes, add 4 lamb kidneys which have been split, the tubes removed, cut in fairly small pieces, and soaked in frequently changed cold water for two hours. Simmer the kidneys and vegetables in the stock for a quarter of an hour, and then add 3 tablespoons of chopped fresh dill and salt and freshly ground pepper to taste. If fresh dill is not available, use about ⅔ cup of finely chopped dill pickle. But make sure that the pickle is a good one, tasting more of fragrant dill than of salt and vinegar. Serve the soup smoking hot with a spoonful of sour cream.

A simple, homely Russian soup that is surprisingly good is spinach soup. It is made by adding 1 coarsely diced potato to 6 cups of stock. When this has cooked for ten minutes, a cupful of fresh chopped spinach is thrown in. It is well seasoned with salt and pepper and simmered for about eight or ten minutes. Then half a hard-boiled egg is placed in each hot serving plate and the soup is ladled in and eaten with the addition of a little sour cream.

A good accompaniment to all these soups is black *soldaten* bread. Crisp crusted French is also suitable and delicious. Crackers or "store" bread are not worthy of such noble company. The Russian takes his soup and good bread as seriously as he does his beloved tchai!

Salt and pepper are very important in good soup—salt and pepper that have been added in the cooking. You must season, stir, taste, and then do it all over again, until you have perfection.

The marrow that Katish had so carefully scraped from the bones after half an hour's simmering was used for delectable sandwiches. Thin, crisp whole wheat toast makes a good base. The marrow is heated thoroughly in just a little of the stock and spread thickly on the hot toast. It must be generously salted and peppered—freshly and rather coarsely ground pepper is almost a must! These sandwiches may be served piping hot with the soup. But try cutting them into small squares, sprinkling with dill, and serving with icy dry martinis. No man who remembers his mother's kitchen will scorn this tidbit. (By the way, if a good martini is difficult to manage, pretty good vodka is usually obtainable, and it makes an admirable substitute.)

Mother often featured the soup tureen at Sunday suppers. As a rallying point, it is second only to the cocktail shaker.

Katish's thick split pea soup, rich, savory, and filling, was a favorite for buffet service. It was so thick it did not present the hazards that thinner soups do for lap eating. But it once gave us a breathless moment for all that.

Aunt Martha had a very full social life which had a way of spilling over into our Sunday night supper parties. Her acquaintances were numerous though her standards were exacting. To be really accepted by Aunt Martha you had to be well endowed—worldly goods would do; great erudition was sufficient passport if accompanied by good manners; professional success was creditable; but a good old family name was the thing most esteemed by her. Probably few people cared whether Aunt Martha approved of them or not, but she thought they did, and her steam-roller methods made it difficult for them to avoid the accolade once she had made up her mind to accord it.

For the most part she drew a firm line between the numerous recipients of her charitable assistance and the people who "really counted." Little Mr. Nicolai Krasnoperov was an exception. And the frequency with which she brought him to our Sunday suppers, the time she spent learning to cook the things he liked, had convinced us that she might be thinking of him as more than an acceptable acquaintance.

But our speculations hadn't received any real proof. And when, Sunday after Sunday, for more than a month, we saw nothing of the gay little man, we began to believe we had been mistaken. Aunt Martha now shepherded to our suppers an Austrian obstetrician who was all the rage in Los Angeles that winter. She had always told Mother that it would do us children a world of good to meet the cultured people she moved among. I don't think Mother quite understood how we were to benefit by the presence of an obstetrician at that late date, but Aunt Martha's guests were made welcome, and Mother never said anything to her sister-in-law about the well-understood facts that her own apartment was rather small for entertaining, and anyway, she hated to cook.

The obstetrician was an odd-looking man, tall and very thin, with a sharp little mustache and a Van Dyke beard stretching out an already too long face. Distinguished looking, Aunt Martha said. Bob and I pointedly remarked that he wasn't half so amusing as Mr. Krasnoperov—our adored Mr. Redfeather. But Aunt Martha held her own counsel and continued to bring the doctor to supper until the fatal evening of the pea soup.

That night we also had as a guest a very beautiful young woman with a very fine figure which she did not hesitate to display. At this simple supper party she wore a black semi-evening dress cut wondrously low in the neck. Mother ladled out the pea soup and the young lady and the Austrian doctor took their trays to a sofa together. They seemed to be enjoying both each other and the soup immensely. The young lady flashed her big eyes at the doctor and held her spoon poised in mid-air. At that moment someone passed around the sofa and joggled her elbow! Splash! went the pea soup, right on the lovely lady's daringly exposed white bosom.

Quick and neat as a cat the Austrian doctor licked his spoon, deftly scooped up the blob of thick soup from the lady's now agitated person, and went on calmly eating his own soup! The rising tide of a rosy blush had not time to engulf the little pea-green island before it was swept away. The embarrassed young woman hadn't even time to get her napkin from under the tray in her lap before the incident was finished.

But Aunt Martha left early and alone and thoroughly scandalized. Her little electric seemed to simmer with the indignation of its owner as it pulled away from the curb. When she got home she lost no time in calling up all her expectant friends, and all those who might reasonably expect to become expectant and telling them what a horrid creature the popular obstetrician had turned out to be. The next Sunday evening found Nicolai Krasnoperov at our house, contentedly eating borsch and singing his Russian songs that sounded as gay and untroubled as ever.

KATISH'S PEA SOUP

Put 4 cups of dried green split peas with 3 quarts of water into a large, heavy kettle. Add 1 large onion, cut in slices, ¼ pound of salt pork which has been cut in squares and browned well on all sides, then drained of excess fat, 1 clove of garlic, and 2 carrots. Cook over a low fire, stirring often to prevent sticking, for three hours. By this time the peas should have cooked soft enough to need no sieving, but fish out the chunks of vegetable and put them through a sieve and back into the pot. Add salt judiciously, some fresh black pepper—quite a bit of this—and a bay leaf. Add 2 cups of cream or top milk. Put over a low fire and simmer very gently for about twenty minutes. Add more cream if you want the soup thinner, some moistened flour if you wish to make it thicker. Real pea soup lovers swear that the spoon should stand alone in the bowl! Now take some highly flavored sausage and cut it into rather generous bite-sized pieces. Drop this into the soup just in time to heat through.

If you don't care for the lustier sausages, you can use cubed ham and stir in ½ cup of dry sherry just before taking the pot from the fire. The salt pork and the sausage or ham cubes are served in the soup, of course. Salad and a dessert are all that are needed to complete the meal.

Katish did many wonderful things with mushrooms, and not the least of these was her cream of mushroom soup. It is a meal in itself when served with crusty French bread.

FRESH MUSHROOM SOUP

Wash quickly, dry and slice thinly ½ pound of mushrooms. Melt 4 tablespoons of butter or good quality shortening in a heavy pan. When butter is hot, put in the mushrooms and sauté them to a golden brown. Add a thick slice of onion and sprinkle in 4 teaspoons of flour. When the flour has been absorbed by the fat, gradually stir in 1 cup of beef broth. Then add 2 cups of hot, thin cream, 3 drops of Maggi Seasoning, and a snip of bay leaf. Salt and pepper to taste and leave over low heat for ten minutes, but do not boil. Remove the onion slice and the bay leaf, and serve in warm bowls.

Aunt Martha was not the only one who invited unexpected guests to our house. Katish was incurably sociable. We were a little bewildered when, after her coming, our friends began dropping in at dinner time, quite evidently sure of their welcome and expecting to be royally fed. We puzzled over our suddenly increased popularity until Mother grew suspicious. Katish, she thought, must have a hand in the matter. "*Da—da, da, da*—I invite," Katish admitted cheerfully; in fact, well pleased with herself, she was responsible for the small-scale invasion. Whenever she ran across some friend of the family, she asked them to call. If they happened to be lonely business girls, or better still, pitiful, unloved, unpampered, uncooked-for bachelors, she asked them to dinner.

Mother, after a lifetime of Aunt Martha's example, was not much given to interfering in the affairs of others, but now and then she could not resist giving some backward young fellow a gentle shove toward the bliss of matrimony. For a long time she had been inviting a certain charming bachelor and a shy, nice girl to dinner together from purely subversive motives. After Katish came to us the bachelor spent his evenings in the kitchen helping her to wash the dishes and living again the five weeks in Russia that had been a high point of his existence. Reluctantly, Mother gave up asking the nice girl. If Katish, wearing an apron and surrounded by dirty dishes, had more charm for the bachelor than the girl had in her prettiest frock with her blond hair set off to advantage by the soft blue upholstery of our living room sofa, it must be admitted that the case was hopeless.

But the bachelor continued to come to dinner, more often than ever. Katish invited him.

We even got to know, after a time, when company was coming, by the bustlingly busy sounds that could be heard from the kitchen. Mother never saw any reason to object, for weren't the cooking and the dish washing up to Katish? And the budgeting, too. Katish was still making out all right financially on her modest food allowance, in spite of her hospitable impulses, as the present of the delightful crackle-ware bowls had recently proved.

CHAPTER SIX

There was always a great deal of sweep and dash in the sight of our jolly Russian cook at her bread and pastry making. She had looked just once at the measly pastry board Mother had pointed out to her when she took over the kitchen. "You not minding I take paint off top?" Katish stroked experimentally the solid old "mission oak" table that had been relegated to kitchen use and masked under cream paint.

Mother said she didn't mind. Katish volunteered no reason for her desire. She went to work with paint remover and scouring materials and soon had the old table top bare and smooth as glass. She touched up the paint on the under part of the table and ran a thin finishing line of bright red around the edge of the top. Then she went happily at her dough and pastry making with all that fine unhampered space to work on.

Here she made the dough for the pirogues and piroshkee (Russian meat and fish pies) that accompanied her wonderful soups. They make splendid everyday fare, and the pirogues, at least, hold a place in festive occasions as well—a traditional and well-deserved place. For the pirogue is the Russian "name-day pie" which rather corresponds to our birthday cake.

Bob's birthday loomed in the offing, and Bob wasn't taking any chances on having the occasion forgotten. He meant to have the biggest and best chocolate cake that he or any of his friends had ever seen. I gallantly helped him out with hints and reminders; after all, I'd be having a birthday of my own before long. Asked what he would like for his birthday dinner in addition to the much-talked-about cake, Bob replied that he wanted the usual fried chicken and ice cream. But, he asked, what was customary for a Russian birthday celebration? Katish explained that among Russians birthdays take second place to name-days. She described the name-day, or *iminini,* pirogue. He thought he'd like that, too. And borsch, of course. And why not a meat pirogue while Katish was about it?

Katish laughed and protested that he couldn't possibly have all that for one dinner. At last a compromise was reached. To Bob's perfect satisfaction it involved the preparation of two birthday dinners, one American, one Russian. He would ask the same guests for both occasions and see which dinner they liked better.

The all-important name on Bob's guest list was that of Helene, a little blue-eyed, blond member of the high school sophomore class. I remarked with sisterly acidity that I couldn't see why he wanted to invite her, for she had only to look at him to reduce him to silent, open-mouthed idiocy. But he not only wanted her at his two dinner parties, he was even willing to sacrifice his tender dignity by going to bed with his unruly hair tightly imprisoned in the sensible cotton top of one of Katish's stockings for a week before the first of the great days. Even my teasing could not shake his resolution to present an appearance worthy of such divine company.

Unfortunately, his efforts were very nearly brought to nothing by an overexcess of manly zeal. Katish had kindly supplied the stocking top in response to his plea for something to help control his recalcitrant locks. "When you going to bed," she counseled, "put first some oil on hairs. (Katish often used the plural in speaking of hair, in literal translation from the Russian.) Then you comb hairs, so-o-o neatly, and put on top from stocking. Will be all fine for party."

Katish's advice was good, so far as it went. But she hadn't said *what* oil to use. It happened that Bob was all out of hair tonic, and anyway, sad experience had destroyed his faith in the preparation he had been using. So he went out to the pantry without saying anything of his intentions and appropriated a bottle of olive oil he found there. Taking the bottle to his room, he proceeded to make nightly use of the contents, until the day of the first party.

At lunch that day Mother looked puzzled and a little distressed. After the meal was over she went out to the kitchen to hold a conference with Katish. "Katish," she asked, "do you know where that strong odor of garlic in the dining room comes from? I've been noticing it for a day or two, and it seems to grow stronger. But I couldn't detect garlic in anything that you served. What can it be? We must get rid of it before our guests come tonight!"

Katish affirmed that no garlic had been used in the luncheon dishes. They went together into the dining room and began looking under and into things. "Why, there's no smell of garlic now!" Mother exclaimed. "How odd. Do you suppose it isn't garlic at all, but something that Bob is carrying around in his pockets? I thought he had outgrown that sort of thing, but perhaps we ought to find out for sure. Sis, go tell Bob to come in here, right away."

I trotted off in search of Bob and found him on his back under The Menace.

"Ai, *da*, is from Bob, that smell!" Katish exclaimed as she came into the room.

"Bob Thurston," Mother ordered, "turn out every one of your pockets this instant and let me see what you are carrying around that smells so frightful."

"Why, I'm not carrying anything," Bob protested. "What do you think I am, a little brat who carries mouse tails to scare silly girls?" With an air of deeply offended dignity he complied with Mother's demand.

Just behind Bob stood Katish, inspecting closely the pile of objects that he placed upon the table. Suddenly her black eyes gleamed, she stood on tiptoe and sniffed once. Quickly she stepped back.

"Is not the things in pockets. Is hairs that smell!" she announced sternly. "And now I know where is bottle of olive oil with garlic that I am keeping to make spiced olives."

"Oh, Bob," Mother moaned. "Have you taken Katish's olive oil? Then it serves you right. You know you aren't supposed to take things from the pantry without asking. Now you'll have to shampoo your hair, thoroughly and immediately, and what it will look like tonight, I refuse to contemplate."

Bob looked crestfallen. After all his efforts, to have this happen! But, he finally admitted, Mother was right. He couldn't sit next to the devastating sophomore smelling to high heaven of olive oil and garlic.

Mother went off to the bathroom with Bob. I was dispatched on my bicycle carrying a note to the friendly druggist down the block. Bob spent the afternoon indoors, wearing an application of the hair oil recommended by the druggist and a new stocking cap quickly fashioned by Katish. By evening his hair had been persuaded into a reasonably amenable mood, and he smelled rather strongly of lavender. Probably *la belle* Helene would admire the fresh, clean scent, Mother comforted him. And, due to certain events in my own life of the past week, I wasn't in a position to make anything conversationally of the near-disaster at the party. Silence for silence would be the rule between Bob and me for some time to come.

The American dinner party was a great success; such quantities of fried chicken, ice cream, and chocolate cake were consumed by the family and Bob's guests that it was deemed wiser by Mother to hold the Russian party several days later to give Katish time to recover from the efforts of preparation and the rest of us a chance to recover from our enjoyment.

Still, the double celebration seemed to Mother a reasonably small effort after the single regulation "children's party" that had been held in former years, when she had had to cope with a dozen or so of assorted boys whose separate and combined determination seemed to be to do nothing that would look sissy—in other words nothing quiet, sane, and understandable to the adult intellect. Most of Bob's guests this year were grown-ups; and Bob himself was put on his best, most dignified behavior by the presence of his beloved.

The Russian dinner began with canapés of smoked salmon and salmon egg caviar. Then Mother passed around plates of beautiful red borsch. Katish brought in the *iminini* pirogue and placed it before Bob. As his knife went through the tender puff paste to the filling of fish, rice, eggs, and savory seasonings, the Russians among our guests looked very pleased. Their smiles grew even wider as Katish bore to the table another great rectangular pie, this time with a delicate yeast pastry crust and a meat filling. The fish pie is the true *iminini* pirogue, but since Bob was unorthodox enough to celebrate a birthday, rather than a name-day, Katish saw no reason why he should not have both.

Boris Antonovich Nikitin explained to Helene the use of the Russian middle name which, to the utter mystification of the uninitiated, always seems to end in *vich*! "Russian names are really simple," Boris Antonovich said, "once you know the rules. It's like this: At his christening every Russian child receives a first, or given, name, just as one does in America. But this name which is given to the Russian child is that of some saint of the church. The child will celebrate as his name-day the day set aside in the church calendar as belonging to his particular saint, the one for whom he has been named. This is true also in Roman Catholic countries, like Mexico.

"Then, in addition to this given name, the Russian child automatically receives a middle name which is the first name of his, or her, father. This middle name is the patronymic. For a girl, it has one ending, for a boy, another form of ending, meaning *daughter of* or *son of*, as the case may be.

"So, you know from my middle name, Antonovich, that my father was Anton. And that my sister, Olga's, middle name is Antonovna. When I have children and they are christened in the Russian Church, they will all be Nina Borisovna, or Dmitri Borisovich, and so on, because I am Boris."

Russians who came to the house and were not close friends of Katish always addressed her as Ekaterina Pavlovna. We should have had to think for a moment if anyone had asked us her family name, so seldom was it used. Among Russians, it is proper to use the first name with the addition of the patronymic at first meetings.

The Russian custom of celebrating the name-day, rather than the birthday, seems to have its advantages. For one thing, one's friends have less trouble in remembering the date. They have only to glance at a Russian calendar at the beginning of each month to see which of their friends must be congratulated or remembered with presents. And then that depressing feeling that still another year of our stingy few has gone comes with less force when there is no necessity to perform the simple but inescapable feat of arithmetic involving the addition of 1 to —?

There are several schools of thought on the subject of pastry for pirogues. Some believe that a rich flaky pastry is best, others regard a tender yeast pastry as supreme. The third choice is a real puff paste.

NAME-DAY PIROGUÉ

Line a square tin, about 1½ inches deep, with your chosen pastry. Cover the bottom with a thin layer of cold boiled rice. Over this sprinkle a layer of lightly browned chopped green onions. Then put in a layer of chopped hard-boiled egg. Next a somewhat thicker layer of any good white fish which has been gently poached in a little water seasoned with bay leaf, a slice of onion, salt, and some peppercorns. The fish should be moist and broken into small chunks, but not flaked. On top of the fish, put some onions, then a layer of chopped eggs, then more rice. Repeat this until the pan is full, seeing that each layer is properly seasoned with salt and pepper. Sprinkle a little of the fish bouillon over the filling and dot with butter. Then seal on the top crust and pierce with a fork. Bake in a hot oven, 425°, until the crust is cooked and brown.

MEAT PIROGUE

Brown a large onion or 1 bunch of chopped green onions in 1 tablespoon of fat. Add more fat and cook 1 pound of ground beef lightly, letting it brown a little, but not allowing it to dry out. Chop two hard cooked eggs. Arrange meat, onion and eggs in layers in a pastry lined square tin (this will fill a tin nine inches square by 1½ inches deep), and seal on top crust. Pierce with fork and bake at 425°.

PIROSHKEE

Piroshkee are small individual pies served with soup. They may have the meat filling described above or as in Chapter Four, or a mixture of sautéed mushrooms, rice, egg, and onion; or they may be filled with chopped egg, browned onion, and lightly sautéed chopped cabbage. They may be made with puff pastry, flaky pastry, or best of all, the yeast dough.

The first two types of pastry must be baked, of course, but the yeast dough may be either baked or fried. The little fried piroshkee are delicious. For sweet pies, try filling them with cooked dried apple or apricots and rolling in powdered sugar to be eaten while hot.

YEAST PASTRY

Heat 1 cup of milk and pour it over 4 tablespoons of shortening, 2 teaspoons of salt, 3 tablespoons of sugar. Cool to lukewarm and add 1 fresh yeast cake, finely crumbled. Add 1 cup of flour and beat thoroughly. Add 2 beaten eggs. Then work in just enough flour to make a very light dough; it will take about 2 cups, perhaps less.

Knead until elastic on a floured board, taking care that you do not work in more flour than necessary; this dough must be light. Put in a warm place to rise for six hours. Then roll out fairly thin on a floured board. Cut in small rounds, no bigger than the top of a water glass. Put some filling in the center of each and seal the edges very carefully with milk. Let the piroshkee stand on the board in a warm place for twenty minutes. Then fry them until well browned in deep, hot fat, or bake in a hot oven. Serve at once. This recipe also makes a fine crust for the large, baked pirogues.

The recipe for Katish's easy-to-make puff pastry has already been given. Her flaky pie pastry can be used for pirogues, piroshkee, or for a delicious American apple pie. It is the best all-round pastry recipe that I have found, and it makes no lavish use of butter, but substitutes sour cream for a goodly portion of the butter that would otherwise be required.

KATISH'S FLAKY PASTRY

Sift together 1½ cups of all-purpose flour, 1 teaspoon salt. Cut in ¼ cup of butter, leaving the mixture in coarse lumps. Add cold sour cream, about 6 tablespoons, but a little at a time, so that you do not add a bit more than necessary to hold the dough together. Use no water at all. Roll out the dough, fold in three thicknesses. Put into refrigerator for half an hour or more, then roll to desired thickness and bake in a 425° oven.

My sisterly disrespect for Bob's obvious subjugation by the lovely Helene was somewhat mitigated when I saw that size nine blond competently tuck away two plates of Katish's good borsch and generous slices of both the fish and meat pirogues and then top it all off with the rich Charlotte Russe that had been Bob's choice of dessert, and after only a moment's hesitation, a dainty crystal dish of the fresh fruits in liqueur and plain cake that Mother had provided for the less ferocious appetites of her grown-up guests. Helene's delicate, ethereal appearance, which was the envy of her schoolmates, couldn't be held against her, I decided, when she so evidently took no pains to preserve it. She was all right, even if she didn't seem to mind the spoony way Bob looked at her.

My understanding of the gentle passion appears to have been a bit on the retarded side. I knew, of course, that even some of the boys and girls of my own class did a bit of mooning about, and considerable hand-holding in the movies. But hand-holding didn't go with the kind of blood and thunder movies I still preferred. And as for teen-age boys, they were a long way from being objects of hero-worship to me. I hadn't had a brother about all these years for nothing. Boys, I knew very well, were considerably less romantic than Tom Mix's horse. What, for instance, would the dainty Helene have thought of Bob if she could have known about the garlic in his hair? And that, though he was sixteen now, he still couldn't be trusted to give his little sister the larger share of the delicious "try-cake" that Katish usually made for us? And most terrible of all, that he wasn't even above telling tales on that poor little sister when it suited his purpose?

When I saw Bob giving Helene one of those calflike looks I was sorely tempted to tell about the garlic, but I knew what would happen if I did. Bob would relate my own most recent disgrace. And if that story got to the ears of Aunt Martha, I wouldn't get the five dollars that she always gave us for our birthdays. Bob had his now, and was safe for another year. But it was still three months to my birthday.

It was my own inability to appreciate those calf looks from the opposite sex that had put me in this deplorable position to be blackmailed into silence.

For quite a long time, Mother had been receiving visits and invitations from a middle-aged widower named Mr. Powers, who had first been brought to the house by Aunt Martha. I didn't like the way Mr. Powers looked at Mother, though I found some comfort in the calm way in which Mother looked at *him*. Above all, I didn't like Mr. Powers' anemic son, Walter. Walter was a very polite boy, but he just couldn't bring himself to admire or to ride in The Menace. His father owned a big black sedan which I once told Walter looked like a bootlegger's car. He only shrugged at my rudeness and told me the horsepower of the big sedan. Bob couldn't stand Walter and, since he had a good deal more freedom of action in the evenings than I did, he usually managed to escape, leaving me to do the honors when Walter came to call with his father.

A few days before the birthday dinner, the Powers, *père et fils,* had glided up one evening after dinner, in the immense, silent black sedan. Bob promptly thought of a date with a fellow. Mother and Mr. Powers played over some new classical recordings in the living room, and I attempted to bore Walter into an unshakable resolution never to come again. We sat on the porch and carried on a largely one-sided conversation in which he offered various suggestions for my entertainment. I refused them all disdainfully—even the lovely cowboy movie that was playing near-by.

I sat in the big porch swing, pushing myself back and forth violently and looking stubborn. Master Walter sat on the steps, talking politely and valiantly against my unhostess-like attitude. Finally he got up and sat down with me in the swing.

"I don't see why you don't like me," he complained. "I do everything I can to be nice to you." He put a tentative—and even well-scrubbed—hand over mine, and gave me one of those sickening looks. In a split second Master Walter was lying flat on his back on the stone porch, and I was seated firmly astride his stomach, my knees gripping his scrawny ribs while I savagely pounded his skull on the unyielding floor. It made a lovely, satisfying sound. But it was a little disappointing that he wouldn't yell for help. Later, I couldn't decide whether it was his gentlemanly code that kept him silent, or simple stupefaction.

But just then Bob drove by in The Menace and stopped with a wild shrieking of brakes and rattling of insecure fenders which brought Mother in terror to the door. Mr. Powers strode behind, ready to give reassurance or to prove himself capable of decisive action in time of emergency.

He stopped, dazed, when he saw it was his own son who needed succor. Mother used her sharpest reprimand. She addressed me by my full name—that awful, unspeakable name that Aunt Martha had marked me with! "Get up instantly and apologize to Walter," she demanded firmly.

It seemed best to do as Mother said. After all, Walter, if consciousness still prevailed, now had a terrible weapon to use against me—that name! Walter proved himself every inch a young gentleman. He got unsteadily to his feet and straightened his tie.

"It's all right—Sis," he said, and I breathed again. "I had it coming, I guess, Mrs. Thurston."

"Gosh all fish hooks!" Bob rejoiced when we were alone. "I didn't know you had it in you, Sis. I've been wanting to do that to that little Powers worm for months, but I couldn't because he's such a skinny runt it wouldn't look right. But since you're just a girl, it doesn't matter. Boy, oh boy, it was wonderful!"

"I've never been so much ashamed of one of my children," Mother said sorrowfully.

I tried to get some sympathy from Katish, but she was ashamed of me too. And what Aunt Martha would say if she heard of it, was too awful for conjecture. Mr. Powers was a great friend of hers, and a man of wealth and considerable importance in the city. He didn't come to our house so often after that and when he did he looked alarmed whenever I came into the room, as if I might fly at him, given the slightest provocation.

Much as Bob approved my pugilistic accomplishment, I knew full well that he wasn't above giving me away to Aunt Martha before my own birthday if I dared to make public the reason for the strong aura of lavender which pervaded the birthday party.

In the voting for the best dinner—Russian or American—that closed the double celebration, the Russian dinner won by one vote. But that may have been only because it was of more recent memory.

CHAPTER SEVEN

Katish was making cinnamon buns when Uncle William arrived for his yearly visit. And since Uncle William was a man who decidedly knew a good thing when he smelled it, he took himself straightway to Katish's kitchen.

When Mother and I got home from meeting the train that my great-uncle didn't arrive on, we found him cosily ensconced in the breakfast nook, beatifically devouring the very last of that batch of cinnamon buns and drinking strong hot tea while he followed Katish's plump, busy figure with an appreciative, more than middle-aged eye.

I didn't feel too happy at the sight of that last sugary bun disappearing from view. It was bad enough to get dressed up and go all the way to the station only to learn that our visitor had arrived on an earlier train without bothering to let us know. It did seem that Katish might have thought to hide a few of those good fresh buns away for me. But then, I reflected bitterly, there was nothing so touching to the heart of our Katish as a hungry, neglected bachelor. With a childish desire to embarrass both Katish and Uncle William, I recalled one of her frequent sayings.

"He who takes the last must kiss the cook!" I pointed an accusing finger at Uncle William.

"Who ever heard of such a thing?" my imperturbable uncle wanted to know. "Taking the last of anything is only dangerous for girls—it means they'll be old maids. And you'd better not forget it, young lady."

"Tell him, Katish," I insisted. "You know you always tell Bob and me that. It's what the Russians say," I explained as Katish remained silent. "I think it's a much better saying than ours. And I don't think it's fair for you to eat up all Katish's buns and then refuse to abide by the rules."

A speculative gleam appeared in Uncle William's eyes. But just then Mother came back from laying aside her hat. She and Katish joined forces to send me upstairs to pick up the things I'd left strewn about my room when I dressed to go to the station.

Uncle William's visits were made, he said, out of a sense of duty to see that his grandniece and nephew were growing up properly to be a credit to the family. Bob once asked Mother whether Uncle William was a credit to the family. Mother said she'd never thought about it, but probably he was; he had become a rich man through his own efforts.

Bob and I were surprised to learn that our relative was rich. We had always supposed he came to spend a part of each winter with us because it was cheaper than staying at home. For a time, I think we each secretly considered behaving like little angels during his visits so that we might be suitably rewarded at some future day by finding ourselves sole inheritors of his wealth. But, on due reflection, it didn't seem worth while. In early years it always seems easier to make one's own fortune than to be really docile for any long period of time. And our uncle's visits were inclined to be long ones—even by old-fashioned standards of hospitality.

While Uncle William openly deplored Mother's extravagance in keeping a cook, he couldn't conceal the fact that he thought Katish a wonderfully good cook. I overheard Mother's remark to a friend that she was afraid that he was beginning to regard Katish as a "damn fine woman" as well. Uncle William used expressions like that.

When Aunt Martha heard of his growing interest in the kitchen regions she was horrified. "You don't really think he imagines he's in love with your cook?" she fumed.

"It's difficult to associate such an emotion with William," Mother told her. "But I think Katish has too much sense to want him. So I wouldn't worry about her if I were you."

"Worry about Katish! Why, it's William I'm worried about," Aunt Martha retorted. "How can you be concerned about your cook when your own uncle is in danger of marrying a servant?"

"I refuse to worry about either of them," Mother answered practically. "I'll go to the wedding if there is one and I'm asked. But for Katish's sake, I do hope there isn't going to be a wedding."

Uncle William stayed on all through the winter and well into the spring. He enjoyed Katish's cooking so much that he had to order new suits. That looked as if he meant to go on enjoying her cooking. Did he intend to take up his permanent abode with us, or was matrimony in his mind? We couldn't tell. With grudging eyes we watched our not-too-welcome visitor devour the lovely products of Katish's genius. Though she held her own counsel, we felt that she sympathized with us, for after a time, she began to hide away for us plates of fragrant sweet buns, or some other favorite tidbit that might prove irresistible to his robust appetite.

Katish used to say that you could make a home of a hovel by filling it with the fine smell of baking bread. I think she was right, and it is a pity that most women feel that yeast breads are too difficult to prepare. Katish could turn out a pan of crisp, fragrant rolls, and a batch of tiny, spicy cinnamon buns in less than thirty minutes' working time. Of course, there is the rising time to allow for, but you can do what you will with that time.

The most important thing in making yeast breads is to get the feel of good dough. Once you know by the feel when enough flour has been added, when sufficient kneading has been done, and when the mass has risen to a suitable lightness, you will have no trouble with yeast bread and rolls. It just takes a little practice to gain this knowledge. Stick to one good, simple recipe and repeat it until you get it right. You'll have the trick forever after—just as in learning to ride a bicycle! And the preliminaries won't be so painful; in fact, your first efforts will probably result in some fairly pleasant eating.

HOT YEAST ROLLS

Scald a cup of milk. Put into a good-sized bowl 1½ teaspoons of salt, 3 tablespoons of butter or vegetable shortening, and 3 tablespoons of sugar; pour the hot milk over them. When the mixture has cooled to lukewarm, add 1 crumbled fresh yeast cake. Stir in 1 cup of flour and beat thoroughly. Now, if you wish, add 1 beaten egg. This will give a slightly crunchier crust to your rolls, but it is not necessary—simply a matter of preference.

Add flour to your mixture to form a soft dough. Work it up into a ball, using as little flour as possible. With the egg it will take about 2 more cups; without, a little more than 1 cup. The amount of flour will depend upon the texture of the flour itself, the size of the egg, and the temperature of the mixture when flour is added. So don't just dump the whole amount in at once and find yourself with a stiff, sticky mass.

Take the ball of dough from the bowl and knead it smartly on a floured board. Keep your hands and the board lightly floured, but don't work more flour into the dough than you must. When you have kneaded for about five minutes, the dough will begin to feel alive, elastic. Little bubbles may begin to appear on the surface. Put it back into the bowl, lightly oil or butter the top of the ball, and cover the bowl with a clean cloth. Stand the bowl in a warm place and allow the dough to rise unmolested for three hours.

After the dough has risen, take it out onto your floured board. Roll it out about ½ inch thick. Use half of it for plain rolls, the other half for cinnamon buns. To make the plain rolls, cut the dough in ½ inch wide strips and braid 3 strips together. Cut the braids in short lengths, pinch the ends together. Or, tie a loose knot in each strip (the strips for this should be about 6 inches long) and tuck the two ends through the hole in the knot. Bake these last in small muffin pans, well greased. Brush the tops of all your rolls with melted butter, cover the pans with a clean cloth, and put them in a warm place to rise again. This rising will take at least thirty minutes, but the rolls will be better if you allow them about forty-five minutes' rising time. Bake in a 400° oven for about twelve minutes.

CINNAMON BUNS

While the plain rolls are rising, spread the remaining sheet of dough with soft, but not melted, butter. Dust on brown sugar, about half a cupful; sprinkle generously with seedless raisins and cinnamon. Roll the dough up as tightly and evenly as you can. Take a sharp knife and cut off tiny rounds—about 1 inch thick. Place the rounds, cut side down, of course, on a buttered baking pan. Lay them close together, but leave a little room at one side of the pan for the buns to expand into. If you place them apart, they may come unrolled as they rise.

Cover the pan with a cloth and set it in a warm place for about thirty to forty minutes. Just before baking, pour over the buns half a cup of syrup—the kind you use on waffles. Place them in a 400° oven for six minutes, then increase heat to 425° for another six minutes. Remove from the pan while they are hot so that they do not stick. And eat them while they are hot, too!

You will find that yeast dough is not half so temperamental as it is supposed to be. Learn to work with as little fuss and as few dishes as possible, and you'll find yourself making fresh rolls once or twice a week as a matter of course. People who live in city apartments should get the habit; that wonderful warmly welcoming smell can take the curse off even marble halls.

Uncle William consumed truly prodigious quantities of Katish's tender rolls. Mother swore that he could smell them baking five miles away and he always came on the run in time to enjoy them while they were hot. But his love for hot rolls was as nothing compared to his passion for blini—those delicate buckwheat cakes for which the Russians are famous. While Uncle William was disposed to regard all "danged foreigners" with a chary eye, he was broadmindedly willing to admit that some of them did know a thing or two about good food.

Once during Uncle William's visit we had a Frenchman to dinner. There were other guests and it was supposed to be a fairly formal occasion—as formality went in our house. It was seldom that we solemnly gathered around gleaming damask, twinkling candles, and the best silver dazzlingly polished. Such occasions made Katish unhappy. It was nearly impossible for her to pass around the table in the silence which is proper to the well-trained servant. She simply had to lean over a shoulder now and then to recommend some particularly successful dish. If Russians were among our guests, she couldn't resist speaking to them in their own tongue, just to make them feel at home, I guess.

Before the Frenchman arrived, Mother spoke to Uncle William and, as tactfully as possible, requested him not to keep a too openly anxious eye on the silver.

True to form, he grunted something about blasted foreigners all over the place.

"Katish is a foreigner, William," Mother reminded him.

"Katish is different. I don't mind her," he answered serenely from behind his newspaper.

"You'd be surprised to find how many of them are different," Mother informed him crisply, "if you'd only give yourself an opportunity to know them."

"Not the kind of opportunity I'm interested in," Uncle William muttered into the financial page.

Our Frenchman spoke little English and he seemed inordinately shy about expressing himself in the few words he possessed. Mother was mortified to discover how rusty her French had grown with years of disuse, and none of our other guests was proficient enough to carry on a real conversation. It looked like a stalemate. But Uncle William was blissfully unaware of anything strained about the atmosphere. He was tucking away blini with an absorption that at least precluded his assuming an insultingly watchful attitude toward the guest of honor.

Then our valiant Katish, seeing the situation and nothing daunted, turned over the kitchen to the helper who had been engaged for the evening and stationed herself firmly in the dining room, blandly avoiding Mother's surprised glance. As she passed about the table, bringing plates and removing them, she kept up a rapid-fire conversation with the Frenchman in his own language—or rather an imperfect but devastatingly uninhibited facsimile thereof. The Frenchman, relieved of the painful necessity of struggling in an unfamiliar tongue, shot forth streams of Gallic eloquence and enjoyed himself hugely.

At length he took out a little black notebook and began jotting down recipes which Katish supplied. She earnestly supplemented her linguistic talents with such vividly descriptive use of eyes, lips, and hands that the other guests forgot to eat or talk while they watched in breathless fascination. One young woman said she was sure that she had learned more from Katish's illustrated lecture than she had in four years of a domestic science course—and she didn't understand a word of French!

But Uncle William wasn't forgetting to eat. He finished his dainty serving of blini and caviar and began signaling to Katish for another plateful. Katish was genuinely unaware of his distress. But Mother caught his eye. "The blini are only a first course tonight," she told him with gentle firmness.

What with Mother's rebuff and Katish's neglect, Uncle William felt himself a deeply wronged man. And it was obvious that he regarded the foreigner as the source of his troubles. He sat up very straight in his chair while the plates were being changed and glared unremittingly at this guest for whom Katish exhibited such solicitude. But by now the ice was so thoroughly broken that you could have used it for a daiquiri. Mother and her guests forgot their embarrassment over their strangely assorted accents and chatted genially in French, only laughing when they bogged down in their own grammar. The Frenchman reciprocated with his few words of English and Uncle William was allowed to sulk, undisturbed by the gaiety that flowed around him.

I could sympathize with my uncle's desire for more of those delicate blini—when properly made they are so delicious that it seems a shame to stop with two or three. If they are served as a first course, they should be very small and thin. They should always be piping hot, and served on hot plates. You must pass a dish of melted butter, another of sour cream, and whatever your heart desires for topping. You may cover your blini with butter or sour cream or both, then top it with a spoonful of fresh caviar. You can't possibly do better than that! Or you may serve thin slices of buttery, unsalted smoked salmon. Good smoked salmon is rare, but it can be unearthed in most cities, and in the course of the search, who knows what other gustatory treasures may come to light? You will soon learn to recognize really good salmon by its pale apricot color and smooth, buttery texture. It should never be dry or reddish in color.

Then there is red salmon egg caviar. And the delicate filets of herring in wine that are obtainable almost anywhere.

Tiny glasses of vodka should accompany the blini and appetizers. Even if you imagine that you don't care for so fiery a liquor you will find it delicious with the sharp yet subtle flavors of caviar and salmon and the bolder accent of herring in wine against the blandness of sour cream and the tender buckwheat cakes.

BLINI

Sift 3 cups of white all-purpose flour and 1 cup of buckwheat flour with 1 teaspoon salt. Scald 3 cups of milk and cool to lukewarm. Dissolve ½ crumbled fresh yeast cake in 2 tablespoons of the milk and add to the rest of the lukewarm milk. Then add 2 beaten egg yolks. Add the liquid mixture to the flour, gradually, stirring to avoid lumps. Set aside in a warm place and allow to rise for about three hours. Beat well, then, and put aside again for two hours. Just before baking the blini, beat 2 egg whites stiff and fold carefully into the batter. Bake the blini on a hot, lightly greased griddle just as you do any griddle cakes.

It is an unending source of wonder to me that Russians are not fat and lethargic. Their cuisine is so lavish of butter, cream, eggs. But, amazingly, I know far fewer Russians than Americans who are overweight or must diet to avoid being. And goodness knows Russians are anything but lethargic. Katish said, "Is American state of mind make dieting necessary. You have great lack of curiosity. Good Russian is bursting with curiosity."

Russians *are* full of curiosity—all kinds of curiosity. The purely personal sort, an endless amount of intellectual curiosity, and a great deal of the humanitarian variety. They wonder what makes things go. And they try to find out. They want to know how other people live, how they feel about things. And they inquire. They wonder about their own immortal souls and yours. And they discuss things unceasingly. They want to know the answers to countless abstract questions. And they argue spiritedly. They would like to know how much money you earn and how much rent you pay, and often as not, they ask you! Perhaps all this does require good solid nourishment.

Another type of Russian pancake is a good deal like the paper-thin pancake of Crêpes Suzette. It is much simpler to make than blini, and can be whipped up on a moment's notice from materials that are almost always in any pantry. You will need several tiny, heavy iron skillets if you are going to serve a crowd, for they must be served fresh and hot. These delicate, sweet pancakes are called blintchky. When Katish made them we all took turns in watching the pans and ate the cakes in the kitchen so that they would be at their delectable best. They were given only to those guests who could be counted on not to raise their eyebrows when Mother announced that we would adjourn to the kitchen for dessert. Katish was in her glory then, as she hovered watchfully over the miniature griddles, transferring their fragrant, pure gold contents to the hot plates the guests eagerly held out.

BLINTCHKY

Beat 2 whole eggs and add ½ cup of milk. Mix 2 tablespoons of sugar, ½ teaspoon salt and ¼ cupful of flour together. Stir dry ingredients into milk and egg mixture. Beat enthusiastically for several minutes. Butter pans and heat them. Put a very small amount of the batter into each pan and tilt so that it runs to the edges. Never mind if the cakes are lacy around their edges. Shake over the fire for about two minutes and then turn. The blintchky should be very thin and golden-brown. Serve plain, sprinkled with sugar, or with dark currant jam, or with a Suzette sauce.

SUZETTE SAUCE

To ¼ cup of honey add 4 tablespoons of orange juice, 1 scant tablespoon of lemon juice, and 1 tablespoon of the mixed peels, finely grated. Pour this over ¼ cup of sugar. Then work this mixture into ¼ pound of fresh sweet butter. Store in the refrigerator until needed. Melt sauce in a heavy pan or chafing dish. Add some Cointreau or fine brandy, about 1 ounce. Heat the folded blintchky in the bubbling mixture. Add more brandy and set alight. When the flame has died down, serve the fragrant blintchky immediately on hot dessert plates.

One night after Katish had given us a particularly good dinner, Uncle William followed her out to the kitchen. I could see that Mother was tensely waiting for something to happen so I trotted out to see how things were progressing. All I saw was Uncle William snugly tucked behind the kitchen table, slowly eating another slice of cheese cake. I knew how much he liked it; still, he'd had two slices at dinner. Katish was calmly washing dishes and paying no attention to him. I went back to the living room feeling that this state of affairs would probably continue until Bob and I grew up and established homes of our own. I resolved firmly to hide my culinary talents, if any, from visiting relatives when that happy day came.

Mother couldn't bring herself to hint that Uncle William had overstayed his welcome and he didn't seem able to bring himself to the point of either a proposal or departure. After all, his life was very comfortable as it was. Mother looked up inquiringly as I came in, but I just shook my head gloomily at her.

But then something did happen. Suddenly the air was rent by two sharp shrieks and the clash and clatter of breaking china! Before Mother and I could leave our chairs, a flying blue blur streaked like electricity by the living room door, through the hall, and up the stairs!

"Heavens! what can have happened to Katish?" Mother hurried up the stairs after our agitated cook.

Uncle William came slowly out of the kitchen and strolled over to the window. He was doing his best to look nonchalant, but his face was red, and it was easy to see that he was mad as blazes. I didn't make him any happier by asking, "Uncle William, WHAT have you done to Katish?"

"Not a thing, not one damn, blasted thing!" he exploded, totally forgetful of my tender years. "How should I know that the woman is a raving lunatic? You'd think that a woman who can cook like that would have some sense. Damnation!" He took out one of his evil-smelling, long black cigars and lighted it for comfort. "Tell your mother that I've gone out to see a friend and that I'm catching a train for home tomorrow." He took his hat from the closet under the stairs and strode out the door.

I pelted up the stairs and knocked at Katish's door. Mother came out and drew me back down the stairs. "Leave Katish alone for the rest of the evening," she ordered. "She's had a bad shock. And come out and help me finish the dishes."

"Aren't you going to tell me what happened?" I demanded indignantly. "Uncle William is mad as anything. He's gone out for the evening and he's going home tomorrow!"

Mother looked at me without saying anything for a minute and then she began to laugh. "All right. I'll tell you. But you are sure Uncle William said that he'd leave tomorrow?"

I told Mother that I thought she could depend upon that.

"Well, Uncle William just proposed to Katish. She said she was standing at the sink with her back to him. She'd forgotten all about him when he spoke up. He began by saying that he was thinking of going home, but that he'd miss her cheese cake and cinnamon buns. Katish was very pleased to hear that he wouldn't be staying much longer. She went on doing dishes and Uncle William went on eating cheese cake. She thought he must be stoking up for all his months at home. Then, all of a sudden, he said, 'Will you marry me, Katish, and come home with me?'

"Katish swears it had never occurred to her that Uncle William would think of such a thing. She said she felt as if the devil himself were after her and she dropped a dish and shrieked and then ran away without saying a word. No wonder your uncle William is put out. It serves him right, but don't you let on that Katish compared him to the devil!"

Mother got out the broom and began sweeping up pieces of the Haviland platter that matched the soup plates with pink roses. She didn't seem very sad even though the platter had belonged to her grandmother.

Uncle William proposes!

So Uncle William departed and once again the last cinnamon bun fell to me, the last slice of cheese cake to Bob. We gladly obeyed Katish's saying that he who takes the last food upon the plate must kiss the cook. Katish was a jewel who could not be lured from us. We loved her. And Mother had great joy in reciting the proposal scene to Aunt Martha.

CHAPTER EIGHT

The greatest day of all the year for Russians who remember the old days is Easter. Because the old-style Julian calendar is still used to calculate church holidays, Russian Easter seldom coincides with ours.

I think this rather pleased Mother, for I suspect that she was inclined to feel that our Russian émigré friends' manner of celebration was perhaps a trifle hearty for the occasion. Easter, and Russian Easter, were two quite separate things in her mind. And that left her free to enjoy Russian Easter unhampered by any doubts.

On the eve of Katish's first Easter with us we had gone with her to the midnight service in the tiny Russian church on Micheltorena Street in Hollywood. It is a truly charming little church, complete with onion-shaped dome and set in a garden of plants and trees. The chapel is always full to overflowing and many people stand in the garden, hearing faintly the music of the *a capella* choir and the sonorous chantlike voice of the priest as he reads the special service. The fragrance of incense drifts out to blend with the lovely smell of new-mown grass and the young birch trees sway and whisper gently in the cool night wind.

Everyone is dressed in his best; many wear evening clothes in readiness for the festivities which will follow the service in most homes. The light of candles held by the worshipers is reflected in the jewels and ornaments of women and the gleaming white shirt fronts of their escorts. Some have brought tall, round babas and paskha, traditional Easter foods, to be blessed by the priests. With these they make their way to a long table that has been set out to receive them. After the ceremony they will be reclaimed and taken home to grace their owners' Easter tables. Not a crumb of the blessed food may be wasted; should the tiniest morsel fall to the carpet, it must be picked up and eaten.

In the church, seats are provided only for those who are unable to stand or kneel through the services. So those latecomers who must stand in the garden are perhaps more fortunate than those who find room inside the church. And near the end of the service priests, altar boys, choir, and many of the congregation form a procession which moves slowly three times around the outside of the church, singing as it goes, and bearing the holy icons. This procession commemorates the search for the body of Christ after He was risen from the tomb. On re-entering the church the voices of the choir are raised in the joyous proclamation: "*Christos Voskrese*—Christ is Risen."

A sample of the magnificent beauty of Russian liturgical music can be had from phonograph records made by Feodor Chaliapin and the choir of the Russian Church in Paris before the recent war. It is to be hoped that the new tolerance for religion in Russia will outlast diplomatic necessity and that this great musical heritage may be fittingly revived and preserved.

After that first Easter service Katish had gone to break her Lenten fast at the home of friends. Mother, Bob, and I had gone to our own home, feeling forlorn and left out. Next year, we resolved, there would be feasting and friends at our house.

Katish was delighted that we wanted to have an Easter table. It was to be Katish's evening, Mother warned Bob and me, and we would have to do everything that we could to help her. We readily agreed. Katish invited as many of her own friends as she wished and we added a half-dozen of our American friends.

Mother took over the preparation of meals for most of the week preceding Easter Eve, so that Katish might be free to concoct the traditional dishes for the feast. At the last, Katish made Bob and me work like beavers putting every last leaf into the dining room table and setting out plates and platters and bowls and boxes and bottles of good things for the party. Katish had observed a strict fast on that last day and she laughingly said that if she did all that work herself she would not be able to stand through the service—but she never so much as thought of sitting down.

"I fall down—bang! if I be too tired. And I think I do not arose."

We pitched in with a will, even though we were strictly forbidden to taste.

Mother arranged flowers and put mysterious bottles on ice. Several of the bottles were recognizable as wine, but two were unlabeled and their contents looked like nothing more than water. But a surreptitious sip convinced me that there was more than water in them. Prohibition vodka, it turned out to be—a more or less judicious mixture of pure alcohol and water. One of Katish's unencouraged admirers was responsible for that contribution.

There were wonderful things to delight my hungry eyes. In the center of the big table, intricately painted eggs were nested in green grass circled by graceful ferns. Katish had made the nest by covering a shallow, wide bowl with a layer of absorbent cotton, dampening the cotton and sprinkling a quick-growing grass seed generously over it about two weeks before the party. The cotton was kept moist and the grass sprouted rapidly and lushly.

To one side stood the great pyramid of creamy paskha. A little like French *coeur de la crème,* paskha gets its pyramid shape from the wooden mold in which it is pressed to force the moisture from the cheese. On the other side stood the tall baba, a slightly sweet, breadlike cake about eight inches in diameter and more than two feet high. A dozen eggs had gone into its making. Its tall elegance was capped with a lace paper doily dipped in a snowy mixture of powdered sugar and egg-white, and then gracefully molded over the baba while still damp and pliable. Around the base of the tall cake Katish had placed a wreath of tiny pink garden roses.

At one end of the table stood a great ham, juicy and tender.

Katish had wrapped it in a paste of flour and water so that it might bake slowly without drying out. At the last she removed the paste and rind, scored the fat, decorated, and browned the ham to tantalizing perfection. Two fat ducks, filled to bursting with delicious kasha stuffing, graced the opposite end of the table.

A side table held zakuski—hors d'oeuvres. Delicate smoked salmon, caviar, boneless anchovies, Russian eggplant caviar, cheeses, and tiny pickled tomatoes—all were there.

When Bob saw the finished Easter table with all those tempting things so beautifully arranged, he exclaimed feelingly, "Gosh, I wish Igor were here. I'll bet I could show him a thing or two about spitting now!"

Mother and Katish looked at each other, amazed and speechless. It had to be explained to them that Bob and young Igor had had a spitting contest a few days before and Bob had lost. Now he felt that he had an unlimited supply of ammunition after looking at all those mouthwatering, forbidden dishes!

When we left the church at the end of the long, late night service, Bob and I were so excited that we forgot what Katish had told

us about bringing home our lighted candles. Anyone who succeeds in taking home his Easter candle without letting the flame go out will have his dearest wish granted.

One of our guests did reach the house with his candle flame still courageously flickering. It was Nicolai Krasnoperov—Mr. Red-feather. Aunt Martha had brought him from the church in her electric and she reported that he had knelt on the floor and sheltered the candle as carefully as if he had been some devotee of pagan rites, guarding with his very life the precious symbol of his faith.

To Mother Mr. Krasnoperov confided that he found himself in a quandary. He had two wishes, both equally dear to his heart.

"I am not yet decide," he said uncertainly, looking at the gutter-

Katish's first American Easter – in Russian!

ing flame with apprehension lest it should go out before he had made up his mind which wish to make.

Mother thought she could guess one of his wishes. She didn't think he would need any special dispensation in that case. "I'd just wish for the thing I'd wanted longest, if I were you," she told Mr. Redfeather.

Looking vastly relieved, now that someone had decided for him, he closed his eyes tightly for a moment, wishing very hard. Then he joined in the Easter greetings being exchanged all around him.

The Russian Easter salutation consists of an exchange of kisses on both cheeks, accompanied by the words, "*Christos Voskrese*— Christ is Risen."

"He is indeed!" is the warm response.

Everyone gathered around the zakuski table and the vodka was brought out. Vodka is supposed to be drunk in one quick swallow— a surprisingly easy thing to do when a tidbit of caviar or smoked salmon has cleared the way. Katish had a pair of the dearest little wine cups I ever saw and she brought them out for the drinking of toasts to absent ones. The cups were of silver, heavily engraved in Russian designs. The stem and foot of each could be unscrewed and fitted inside the bowl. Then the two parts fitted together, forming a lovely silver Easter egg. Katish filled one of the little cups with white wine for me and let me drink with her to Tania, her sister-in-law, the person now nearest and dearest in all the world to Katish. She was now in France with her husband and a small son named Alex in memory of her brother. Katish sometimes read me parts of Tania's letters. Some day, she said, she and her family might come to America, for her husband's work took them to many parts of the world. I knew that if Katish could have had a chance to wish upon the candle flame that night she would have wished to see her sister-in-law and her tiny nephew.

Most of the Russians with us had family and friends scattered about the face of the earth and they were a little solemn as they thought of their absent ones. But Mr. Redfeather would not let solemnity prevail on such an occasion. He flew about seeing that everyone was supplied with vodka and good things to eat. Now and then he would pick up his balalaika and play and sing something especially gay for us. There was a catchy song about a duck swimming up a river, but since Mr. Redfeather undertook to sing the song in an impromptu English version, the poor little duck never got very far. He was still struggling dauntlessly upstream when the party broke up a little before dawn.

A young colored woman came in to wash the dishes the next morning while we lay late abed. When we came down to breakfast at noon we were amazed to find Katish up and dressed and looking as bright as a new penny. She was wearing her very best bonnet and the new dress she had made for Easter.

"I go now to make my Easter calls," she told us cheerfully.

In Russia, in the old days, a lady stayed in her own house to receive callers on Easter Sunday. Only the men went out on that day. From morning until late at night they diligently made the rounds of their friends' homes, paying their respects to the ladies who, charmingly dressed, waited to receive them.

At each house a gentleman was urged to sample the paskha, to have just a tiny slice of the baba, to try just a taste of the baked ham, a morsel of crackly roast suckling pig. A glass or two of wine or vodka must accompany these delicious viands, of course! Heroic gentlemen!—when the day's last call had been made, how gratefully (and sometimes uncertainly) they must have hastened to their own homes. How firmly they must have shut their doors upon wifely solicitude as to whether they'd like just a bite to eat, and how lacking in Easter piety must have been their comments if they found the Bromo bottle empty upon the shelf!

But—new country, new customs. Russians abroad still celebrate Easter with gaiety and ceremony. But here the ladies often pay calls with their husbands. It's a great game of catch-as-catch-can. Only a few indefatigable bachelors usually manage to find enough of their friends at home to discover in the evening that their stomachs have turned to lead and their legs to rubber.

My best friend was terribly thrilled when she learned that she had been kissed in Easter greeting at our party by a real live prince. That he was all of sixty and hadn't a *sou* to bless himself with didn't

dash her pleasure. Aunt Martha, too, thought better of our chummi-
ness with Katish's friends when she found that they were apt to be
very nice, even if impecunious, people. Aunt Martha, she would
say for herself, was anything but a snob!

I wondered if she had ever learned what had caused Mr. Krasnoperov to turn pale at her suggestion that he would find a title
useful in his business, but I didn't dare to ask. Mother, feeling sorry
at his obvious distress, had said that we must never refer to the matter again.

I heartily shared my aunt's interest in the Russian nobility;
but in rather a different way. I had formed the habit of borrowing
the Sunday "scandal sheet" of a neighbor's paper. Mother didn't
approve of the colorful presentation that this paper affected.
But I found it far superior to the dull toning down of other
sheets. The pictures were wonderful, the texts hair-raising! With
admirable judgment, the editors had accorded space in the magazine section to a weekly paper-doll coloring contest. I would
bring the paper late on Sunday afternoon, when our neighbors
had done with it, spread it out on the floor, and lower myself on
my stomach for an hour of unalloyed delight. Of course I had to
turn through the pages to find my paper-dolls. That gave me a
chance to cast a quick glance at those lovely pictures. Most of the
thrilling story was on one of the back pages, along with my color
work. And, in those days, often those stories dealt with the fantastic goings-on of the Russian upper classes before they had been
thrown to the four winds by the upheaval of the Revolution.
Their breathtaking loves and licentious lives, as seen through the
eyes of an imaginative reporter who had probably never left his
home city, made fascinating reading.

It was wonderful when one of these stories was printed right
alongside the dolls I was supposed to be coloring. Well, I did color
them, after a fashion. As well as I possibly could without looking at
them. And each week I conscientiously mailed my efforts to the
contest editor. Mother must have felt that her offspring was pecu-
liarly ungifted, for I never won a prize.

You can imagine how interestedly I watched the behavior of any

members of the Russian nobility who came my way. When I tried
to question Katish, with what I considered wonderful tact and sub-
tlety, about their mores and morals, she only looked at me in blank
astonishment. I decided that life in America must have had a sub-
duing effect on their characters.

But I was genuinely glad that they had brought along some of
their more creditable customs. Russian Easter seemed a cut above
ours, even if it didn't provide me with an occasion to appear in a
tableau dressed up in white tarleton with gauzy wings that went
flippity-flop.

If you happen to know a little Russian store, you may be able to
buy one of the wooden molds for paskha. But it is still delicious if
you have to fall back on a new flower pot lined with waxed paper for
a mold. It is the hole that makes the flower pot preferable to your best
fancy mold. So be sure to punch out the hole in the waxed paper.

PASKHA

Put 1 pound of the very dry type of cottage cheese through a fine
sieve. Put 2 hard-boiled eggs through the sieve. Cream ½ cup of
sugar with ¼ cup of sweet butter and add 2 tablespoons of sour
cream. Cut a vanilla bean very fine and stir into the butter and sugar
mixture. Put eggs and cheese together once through the sieve. Then
blend cheese and sugar-butter mixtures well. Add ½ teaspoon of salt
and ½ cup of seedless raisins and a little grated orange peel. Press
into a regular wooden paskha mold lined with an old linen napkin,
or line a clean flower pot with waxed paper and interline with the
napkin. Press the paskha down firmly. Place a saucer over the paskha
and put a weight on the saucer so that the moisture is forced from
the cheese. Set the mold in the refrigerator for at least twelve hours
before serving. Then unmold and serve in small portions.

DUCKLING WITH KASHA

Kasha can be bought in fancy groceries and some delicatessens as
buckwheat groats. Ask for the whole grain variety. You cook the

groats like rice in boiling salted water, using just a little less than twice as much water as cereal. When it is to be recooked as in this stuffing, it needs to be cooked for only twenty minutes. If you wish to serve it plain, as you would rice, put it in the double boiler and let it steam for about forty minutes.

But, for the stuffing, cook 1½ cups of the kasha in 2½ cups of boiling salted water for twenty minutes. Put it into a bowl and add 1 medium-sized onion chopped and lightly browned in butter or drippings, ½ cup of seedless raisins, and ½ cup of chopped walnut meats. Season well with salt and pepper and use as a stuffing for duckling or boned shoulder of pork.

EGGPLANT CAVIAR

Boil a whole, unpeeled eggplant until tender. Cool, peel, and chop fine. Add a finely minced onion, a mashed clove of garlic, 1 chopped, drained tomato, 1 teaspoon sugar, salt and pepper to taste, 2 tablespoons of vinegar, and 3 tablespoons of olive oil. Mix well and chill. Serve on thin buttered slices of rye bread or crisp white toast rounds.

EASTER BABA

Scald 1 cup of milk and cool to lukewarm, then dissolve in it 2 cakes of fresh yeast. Beat 4 egg yolks and gradually add 1½ cups of sugar. Then beat in 2 whole eggs. Melt ¼ pound of sweet butter, and while still warm, add it to the beaten eggs and sugar mixture. Add ¼ pound of seedless raisins, 1 teaspoon crushed cardamon seed, or some finely chopped vanilla bean and a little grated orange peel. Then stir in the milk and yeast. Gradually add 4 to 5 cups of flour to make a soft dough. Knead for ten minutes on a floured board, put back in bowl, and let rise in a warm place for about six hours, or until doubled in bulk. Pound it down, put into buttered forms, and let rise again. Bake at 350° until a straw comes out clean. The time will depend upon the size and shape of the forms you use.

Baba should be tall and cylindrical in shape. The best form for its baking that can be found is an old five-pound coffee tin, lined with waxed paper.

Just before the beginning of Lent, we had observed the three days of feasting that the Russians call Maslianitza, although Katish was the only one of us who proposed to keep the Lenten fast. For one dinner we had had the zakuski and blini, blini, and more blini that are traditional at this time. We had remembered Uncle William's passion for the thin buckwheat pancakes and remorselessly helped ourselves to more.

"It's lucky that no one thought to tell Uncle William that the Russians have a three-day holiday devoted to tucking away enough blini and other rich foods to last them through Lent," Bob remarked. "He'd be with us yet."

"Poor Mr. William," Katish sighed, her cheeks turning pink, and her black eyes softening. Now that he was far, far away, it was safe to be sorry for the old bachelor whose proposal had made her feel that the devil was after her!

During Lent Katish ate no meat at all. One of the dishes on which she sustained herself was tvoroshniki, cottage cheese cutlets. Russians will sometimes eat them as a main course, covered with sour cream and sprinkled with sugar. That, I used to tease Katish, was certainly as bad as putting jam in tea. (No, I still haven't found the Russian who does that.) But I liked tvoroshniki for dessert after a light supper.

TVOROSHNIKI

Put 2 cups of cottage cheese (the dry kind) through a sieve. Squeeze out all possible moisture. Then add 2 tablespoons of sour cream, 2 eggs beaten, 1 tablespoon sugar, 1 teaspoon salt. Add 1½ to 2 tablespoons of flour—just enough to make the mixture stick together. Flour your hands and form into small balls and flatten them so that they are not more than ½ inch thick. Fry in hot butter in a heavy pan. Serve very hot with cold sour cream and a sprinkling of sugar, if desired.

CHAPTER NINE

While she was always modestly deprecatory of her own oddly naïve ingenuity, Katish was admiring and envious of American cleverness and competence. She dearly loved all the gadgets that over-run the American kitchen. Novel can openers and choppers and graters filled her neatly kept cabinets. Her love of such simple mechanical devices was one with which Bob could sympathize and he frequently brought her presents which they eagerly tried out together.

The greatest marvel of all, to Katish, was the automobile. It seemed to her, even after years in this country, wonderful beyond words that mere boys and girls could go whizzing about the highways nonchalantly commanding all that power and speed. Her secret ambition, we guessed, had long been to learn to drive a car. Somehow, she seemed to feel that a driver's license was almost as much a necessary part of her Americanization as her citizenship certificate.

The Menace had long been the only car in the family. Mother was nervously distrustful of things mechanical. Years before she had learned to drive a car—that is, she had learned to drive a car forward. But she had never mastered the art of backing up. And if you couldn't back up, driving became devastatingly complicated.

You had to figure miles ahead, practically, to get where you wanted to go without having to reverse. It just didn't seem worth while. But now Bob was growing up; soon he would be going off to college. And The Menace, he felt, wouldn't fit the dignity of his new estate. He had been working summers and after school, and now he had almost enough money saved to buy a shiny new car. We all assumed that The Menace would form an infinitesimal part of his down payment.

Imagine our astonishment, then, when Bob invited us all one morning to come out and view his old Ford freshly decked out in dark blue paint, all its fenders in place and tightened to a mere rustle in place of the old deafening rattle. That fearful name, too, had been painted out, and in its place, neat and modest letters read BUTTERCUP.

We all breathlessly examined this wonder of wonders and Katish laughed as she spelled out that ridiculous new name. "Is very nice now," she congratulated Bob. "You won't need new car!"

"Oh yes I will, Katish," Bob answered. "The Buttercup is yours! I'm going to teach you to drive. We'll go over to the license bureau and get you a learner's license right away. You can use her for your shopping trips. You won't have to go 'on your foot' any longer!"

So Katish's Americanization progressed. She was an apt pupil, Bob reported. Every morning after breakfast, while the dishes waited, Bob, Katish and The Buttercup traveled several times around the block.

"You just need a little practice, Katish, to give you confidence. I don't have much time to drive around with you," Bob stated importantly, "and you have to have a licensed driver along while you're practicing. How about you, Mother? Isn't that old license of yours still good?"

"Why, yes, I think it is," Mother admitted. "But you know I wouldn't be much help."

"Katish doesn't need any help. I've explained everything to her. You just go along, Mother, to make it all legal."

So that afternoon Katish, with Mother on the front seat beside her wearing her prettiest hat, as she always did when she rode in the old topless car, to soften the dreadful effect, she said, set out to practice. Everything went very well, and before they knew it, they had ventured out on busy Western Avenue. At first Mother was a little nervous, but like most people who don't drive themselves, she didn't worry too much so long as someone else was responsible for getting her to her destination. She just sat still and enjoyed the drive. Katish's expression was extremely earnest, but aside from that, there seemed to be nothing unusual about their progress. Then suddenly, right there on Western Avenue, a strange chugging noise came from the newly christened Buttercup and she began to stagger in the manner of a bloated cow. The earnestness in Katish's eyes turned to alarm, as she strove to control the drunken meanderings of her machine.

"Oh dear, is broken!" she wailed in tones of heartbreak. "What to do?"

"Turn into that garage ahead!" Mother cried. "Bob said something about spark plugs the other day. I don't remember whether he said he'd had them changed, or that they ought to be changed. I don't quite know what spark plugs are, anyway, but the garage man will."

"Aaa-chug, aa-chug," moaned the poor Buttercup as Katish brought her to a masterful halt just inside the garage.

The garage man approached. "Is spark plugs," Katish told him confidently. "You can fix?"

"Sure, I guess so," the man replied. He raised the brightly painted hood and peered under. Then he went and brought some tools and began taking things out and laying them on the fender. Both Mother and Katish felt that it was bound to be all right. A man was in charge now, and didn't men just naturally understand such things? They glanced around the garage, able once more to take an interest in their surroundings.

A man in a green coupé nodded and smiled at them. They looked sternly away. Out of the tail of her eye, Katish thought she saw the man signaling at her. "Is fresh, that man!" she whispered to Mother.

They both sat up very straight and looked in the opposite direction. But loud sounds of merriment coming from the green coupé were too much for them. They stole a look at the man sitting there.

He was laughing crazily to himself. As they turned toward him he again began making those odd signals. "He's out of his mind!" Mother stated firmly. "Pay no attention to him."

The garage man closed the hood with a bang. "She's all right, now. Three dollars, please."

"Was spark plugs?" Katish asked in a business-like way.

"Yeah. Spark plugs," the man assented.

Katish and Mother engaged in a contest to see who should pay the three dollars. Katish said it was her car, so she should pay. Mother said her son had given Katish a present that wasn't in working order, so she was going to pay. In the meantime, the man in the coupé had got out and approached the ladies. He was leaning comfortably over the door on Mother's side before they noticed him.

"Well, girls!" he said, scaring them so that they both jumped a foot in the air.

"Young man—" Katish began in crushing tones.

"Sir!" Mother said haughtily.

"Ha! ha! ha!" the strange man roared. "I oughtn't to tell you, you're so damned highty-tighty, but you'd find it out after you got out on the road anyway. You've got a flat tire! I've been trying to tell you for fifteen minutes, but you wouldn't look at me. Spark plugs, my eye! Don't give this fellow a cent until he's changed that tire for you! Ha! Women! Oughtn't to be allowed on the road!" He shrugged and strode back to the green coupé.

Katish's cheeks were pink with shame as she related their adventure.

"That's all right, Katish," Mother bravely comforted. "It was all my fault. I was the one who said it was spark plugs. And I should have had sense enough at my age to know that that man in the garage didn't want to flirt. But that mechanic really should have known better. It would have saved us all that embarrassment."

Mother was always reluctant to assume responsibility for anything mechanical. She had long wanted an electric refrigerator, but it was not until some bright young salesman explained to her the advantages of the sealed motor type, that needed no oiling and presented no opportunities for amateur tinkering, that she finally bought one.

Katish was heartily glad to be rid of the visits of the impertinent iceman. Not that it was still the same iceman, after all these years, but somehow, the old man always passed on to the new the information that he could get a rise out of Katish by calling her Buttercup. Icemen probably have a dull life at best, *Esquire* to the contrary, so the old joke survived.

Katish's first refrigerator

Katish found the new refrigerator almost as wonderful as her "new" automobile. She related its marvels to anyone who would listen. But there was one thing about it that baffled her. Ours was one of the first models to have an automatic electric light inside, and that light worried thrifty Katish. She didn't like to think of it burning away in there for no good reason. We tried to explain to her that it went out when the door was closed. Her expression said that that was what we thought! She, for one, didn't trust it. She would warily close the door, then suddenly throw it open, as if trying to catch the little light misbehaving. But she was stumped;

there just wasn't any way of knowing what really went on in the box when the door was closed; when it was open the light had a perfect right to burn.

Finally Katish loosened the bulb so that it wouldn't burn at all. Mother promptly tightened it into activity. Katish loosened it. Mother tightened it. This went on for a time and then one day Katish took the bulb out to wash it and "forgot" to put it back. Mother held her peace.

With that fine new refrigerator to hold supplies for unexpected company, Katish encouraged us all more than ever to extend unceasing hospitality. And she never felt the slightest hesitation about inviting any of our friends whom she thought we were neglecting. We might forget all about the Smiths or the Browns for weeks or months, and then suddenly, there they were at our table!

Most Americans, when they first meet a Russian cook, immediately think of shashlik. Katish sometimes made it for our guests, and it was excellent, but she shook her head regretfully as she went about her preparations. It took all of Katish's power of expression to tell what she thought of the American variety of lamb. For didn't it lack the *corduc,* that huge, fur-covered ball of fat, that with the sheep of Turkestan takes the place of the tail and sometimes grows so heavy that it must be supported on a little wheeled platform that the herdsman crudely constructs from the materials at hand? These fantastic sheep, Katish assured us, had a supreme tenderness and juiciness that our lamb lacked. The fat of the *corduc* was used by European Russians as a cooking fat. But the Khirghiz herdsman found it useful in many ways—to oil his saddle, even to grease his gun. By this time, progress being what it is, the lady Khirghiz has probably learned to use it for cold cream.

Once, after we'd eaten our fill of shashlik at a backyard barbecue, Bob remarked, "It wouldn't be a bad idea to make up a few wheeled platforms from the old skates and scooters in the garage so that our guests could wheel their stomachs home in solid comfort, just as the little lambs carry their *corducs* in Turkestan."

SHASHLIK

In a large earthen bowl beat together ½ cup of olive oil, 1 tablespoon of wine vinegar, 1 teaspoon dry mustard, 2 teaspoons salt, 1 teaspoon coarsely ground pepper, 1 tablespoon chopped fresh dill, and a cut clove of garlic. Slice two medium onions rather thickly. Have 3 pounds of boned, cubed lamb. Stir the lamb in the bowl with the marinade and the onion slices; cover, and let stand for several hours. Then string the lamb cubes and onion slices alternately on metal skewers, making sure that the fat sides of the lamb pieces are exposed. Grill to a delectable brown tenderness over hot coals.

Another dish which always seemed delicious to us, although it too had to be made from lamb that lacked the *corduc,* was pilaff. It is one of those recipes which give exceptional rewards for little effort and economical materials.

LAMB PILAFF

To serve six, bone 2 pounds of lamb and cut in cubes. Cover the bones with water and simmer to make a stock. Trim off excess fat from the meat and try it out in a heavy pan or casserole with a tight-fitting cover. Chop a bunch of little green onions fine, using some of the green tops as well as the white globes. Sauté them lightly in the hot lamb fat and then put them aside to drain on brown paper. Then salt, pepper, and dredge the lamb cubes in flour and brown them well on all sides in the fat. Pour over the meat 4 cups of boiling stock you have made with the bones. Add a teaspoon of salt and 2 cups of rice. Cover and bring to a boil, then cook slowly for ten minutes. Now add ½ cup of seedless raisins, 1 cup of grated raw carrots, 3 or 4 halves of dried apricots cut in fine strips, 2 teaspoons of chopped parsley. Stir lightly, cover again, and continue cooking over a low fire for ten to twelve minutes, until rice is just done. Turn out on a hot platter and serve.

Good lamb will be tender after this treatment and it is better not to overcook any meat. But if the tenderness of the lamb used is questionable, simmer the browned cubes for as long as necessary in a little of the stock. Measure the stock remaining in the pot as a part of the 4 cups to be added before putting in the rice.

You will need only a crisp green salad to complete a delicious, satisfying meal.

The ample old cake box that had stood on a kitchen shelf for as long as Bob and I could remember played a part in the ready hospitality which was as natural and as necessary to Katish as breathing. During the winter months, a rich, dark fruit cake, made by a very old Russian recipe, was always stored there, ready to accompany a cup of tea or a glass of wine when callers dropped in. This cake is interestingly different in flavor from ordinary fruit cake, and it keeps well. It should be stored in the usual manner, in a brandy-soaked cloth and a wrapping of waxed paper.

OLD RUSSIAN FRUIT CAKE

Pour ⅓ cup of brandy over the following chopped fruits and let stand several hours: 1 cup of dates, 1 cup of seedless raisins, ⅔ cup candied pineapple, ½ cup citron, ½ cup candied orange peel, 2 tablespoons preserved ginger, 1 tablespoon grated fresh lemon peel.

Put ½ pound of very fat salt pork through the finest knife of the food chopper. Over the pork pour ⅔ cup extra strong, boiling hot coffee. Sift 5 cups of flour with 1¼ teaspoons soda, ⅓ teaspoon each of allspice, cloves, cinnamon and nutmeg. Toss the fruits well in the flour mixture. Now beat 3 whole eggs well and add ½ cup of white sugar, and ½ cup of brown sugar. Stir in ⅓ cup of dark honey, and 1 cup of thick sour cream, and then the cooled pork and coffee mixture. Then gradually beat in the fruit and flour and add 1½ cups of broken, blanched almonds. Bake in a slow oven in waxed paper lined tins. Makes about 5 pounds of cake.

With Katish's very special, rich hot chocolate, we often had a crisp, simple Russian pastry called khvorost (fagots).

KHVOROST

Sift 2 cups of flour into a bowl. Make a hollow in the center of the flour and drop into it 2 egg yolks, ¼ cup of sugar, ½ teaspoon salt, a liqueur glass of vodka, and 1 teaspoon of orange extract—or use rum and vanilla in the same quantities. Work in the flour, roll the pastry thin, cut in small sticks, and fry in hot fat until lightly browned and crisp. Then toss in powdered sugar. These may be kept for some time if stored in a tightly sealed tin.

KATISH'S SPECIAL HOT CHOCOLATE

Put in a small saucepan, over a low fire, 3 squares of bitter chocolate and ½ cup of cold water. Stir until the chocolate is melted, then add ½ cup of sugar and a few grains of salt. Blend well and continue to stir over low flame until perfectly smooth. Take from fire and add ½ teaspoon vanilla. Whip ½ cup of rich cream and fold it into the chocolate mixture after it has cooled. Pour into a small, attractive serving bowl. When ready to use, heat the required quantity of milk just to the boiling point and pour it into a warmed silver pot. Into each cup, put a generous tablespoonful of the chocolate mixture, then fill with the hot milk. This is hot chocolate definitely removed from the nursery class!

Also fine to keep on hand for snacks, and suitable for packing and shipping for an edible gift, as Bob and I learned when we went away to school, were Katish's date bars.

DATE BARS

Crumble 14 graham crackers fine and mix with ½ teaspoon of salt and 1½ teaspoons of baking powder. Add 1¾ cups of chopped dates and 1 cup of broken walnut meats. Beat 3 eggs well and gradually add 1 cup of brown sugar, then beat in the first mixture. Pour into a well greased square pan and bake twenty to twenty-five minutes at 375°. Cut while warm and toss in powdered sugar.

CHAPTER TEN

Our black-eyed Russian cook had always seemed to us the most generous person in the world. We knew that from the salary Mother paid her and the extra sums she received for the fine embroidery which filled much of her spare time, Katish constantly gave help to any of her fellow-émigrés who had found readjustment in their new country difficult. It was seldom that a week passed without some needy soul appearing for a conference with sympathetic Katish. She would take them into the dining room, close the doors, and listen to their troubles over a cheering cup of tea. Occasionally, these people were totally unknown to Katish, but somewhere they had heard of her unbounded willingness to help, and she never let them go away disappointed.

Perhaps, then, it wasn't unforgivable that Bob and I, and even Mother, stared in unconcealed amazement when, one evening, I knocked over Katish's work box and a pile of savings bank books tumbled out! In every color imaginable, ranging from dull buffs and grays to wine-red and turquoise, they lay startlingly revealed against the silvery living room rug!

"Why Katish!" My exclamation was involuntary.

Katish's round cheeks grew scarlet, but she made no answer as she bent in sudden absorption over her needlework. Bob and I knelt to retrieve wildly rolling spools of silk, the gay red darning egg, and, last of all, the scattered little leather books, feeling shocked and embarrassed to have thus surprised Katish's secret. There were seventeen bank books, each with "Ekaterina Pavlovna Belaev" clearly inscribed on its cover! Seventeen! It just didn't seem believable.

We had heard Russians discuss the psychological effects of revolution and turmoil. We knew one man, successful and happy in his life in America, who could not bear to live away from the sight of water—and it must be water that went somewhere, a river that led to the sea, or the sea itself. An inland lake would not do! It must have been the unconscious need to have always before him an avenue of escape that led to this quirk. When it came to money, most Russians we found, had merely had an inborn happy disregard for it intensified. Money was only good, they felt, for the pleasant things it would obtain for themselves and their friends in the present moment. Only a rare few had become hoarders, trying to pile up security for the future. So much could happen, as well they knew, to make such thrift futile!

It didn't seem possible that Katish could be a hoarder. That steady stream of needy callers went away fortified by more than tea and cheerful counsel, we were convinced, though Katish had never told us in so many words that she gave them money. Then what could be the explanation of her seventeen bank accounts?

Katish thanked Bob and me for picking up her belongings and went on with her embroidery, and Mother tried to look as if she hadn't been quite as amazed and curious about those intriguing little books as we!

It was years later that Mother confided to me the secret of Katish's savings. Katish had come to her the next day, Mother said, worried and unhappy. "You are not thinking, Mrs. Thurston," she begged, "that I am miser—that I am like old woman who squeeze every penny and hide away in many places, in case first place not safe? I thought not to tell anyone about bank accounts, but now you know. I am worried you think bad of me."

The explanation that followed Mother's reassurances was highly original, and, as we should have known, highly creditable—an example of Katish's ingenuity and very real kindness. It was true that she gave money constantly to her needy friends. Or, rather, she lent them money. She would have liked to give the money outright, but she had so little, and she needed it, not for herself, but for others. So she had worked out a plan that made repayment easy and unembarrassing for her numerous debtors.

"You know, Mrs. Thurston, if someone owe money, he think he will pay when he has full sum. But that not easy. Something always happen. He meets new pretty girl, or it is his turn to give party for friends. And if money does not come back, I cannot help others. So-oo, I have thought of this; I open account with one dollar in bank which is convenient for each person who owes. When my friend has money to spare—maybe just one dollar—he goes to bank and puts money into account I have there for him. That way he is not embarrass to come with so little. And, after little time, all money is paid into account. My friend cannot take money out again to spend on pretty girl, because account is in my name. If he has again real need, he comes to me, and I give. I think is most simple plan. Banks do bookkeeping for me, and with my friends I need not talk about money. Is all right, you think?" Katish asked anxiously.

"All right!" Mother was ready to burst with pride and admiration for Katish's feminine ingenuity in solving such a problem and letting most of the banks of Los Angeles do a share of her complicated bookkeeping! But Katish had made her promise not to tell anyone.

A further revelation in regard to Katish's bank accounts was that one of those books recorded the borrowings of Julio. All those bambinos of his cost money, and Julio was shrewd enough to realize that Katish, who loved them so, would never be able to resist any plea on their behalf.

"But remember, you Julio," Katish would admonish as she gave him her hard-earned money, "is for babies already here! Not to get more babies. Is thirteen now? Enough, Julio!"

Julio, Katish confided to Mother, wasn't very good about making deposits in his account. But, Katish said, she didn't mind. His failure to repay gave her a hold over the bambinos—a right to insist that they be brought regularly for her inspection and care. Somehow, in spite of neglect, dirt, and heaven knows what diet, they were always fat and bright-eyed and lovable, those babies of Julio's!

We of the family had long since come to look upon Katish as a never-failing source of kindly counsel, and a safe repository for our secrets. I think her advice was always welcome because it wisely took into account human frailty, it was seldom gratuitous, and invariably practical.

My own adolescent aversion to romance had gradually disappeared. I strove as hard as any girl in the school to enliven the hated uniform of white blouse and black tie with a creditable array of fraternity pins. When I bemoaned to Katish the handicap of the goodly crop of freckles that decked my nose, she was prompt to the rescue. "I fix," she promised. And she did, with the aid of the ubiquitous sour cream! She went right out to the refrigerator and mixed up a little pot of fresh, thick sour cream and cucumber juice. Twice a week she made the mixture up for me.

Once when I was red and peeling from a carefree day at the beach, an invitation came for a thrilling party to be given the very next day. I sighed over my reflection in the glass and decided that, at least, I could do something about my hair. I wheedled the price of a new permanent from sympathetic Mother and dashed to the nearest beauty shop. Its nearness was the only thing to recommend that shop—the things they did to my poor hair left me looking like nothing human. But nothing was going to keep me away from that wonderful party.

Katish watched my final desperate primping before the hall mirror. I was bitterly certain that I was going to set a new record for wall-flowers. Katish must have sensed my unhappy thoughts, for she spoke up at last. "When you come to party, just look around carefully and find most handsome boy there. Very good-looking man never notices whether girl is pretty. If he is nice man, he just doesn't think about looks; he's never had to. If he is drog-store cowboy, he is only interested in his own looks. You do as Katish say, and you won't be flower-on-wall. But homely man he always wants to be seen with prettiest girl."

Isn't it true that the handsomest men always marry the plain dowdy little girls and astonish their good-looking rivals by fatuously regarding their wives as world-beating wonders forever after?

I sometimes wished that our wise cook would have a good heart-to-heart talk with Aunt Martha. Maybe she could tell my prickly aunt how to get a husband. There was delightful little Nicolai Krasnoperov, so obviously in need of a good wife to keep him out of the difficulties which his happy-go-lucky temperament got him into. But, while Aunt Martha was undeniably well qualified to take care of any man, she seemed to be definitely lacking in the more subtle feminine qualities—else surely the affair could never have dragged on so long and inconclusively.

Mr. Krasnoperov still came often to our house, usually in Aunt Martha's company. Katish prepared all sorts of Russian dishes for him, and his blue eyes beamed with gratitude and enjoyment. He would tell us stories of Gogol's Patzuik, the redoubtable Cossack who loved vareniki, little cherry dumplings, as much as he did. Patzuik, though, had an inestimable advantage over our Mr. Redfeather. For he had trained his cherry dumplings to jump from the bubbling pot into the bowl of sour cream, thence to his ready mouth!

VARENIKI

The pastry for vareniki is exactly the same as that for pelmeny. But it is cut in 1½ inch squares instead of tiny circles. On one half of the squares you place three or four stoned, sugared black cherries. Then you seal another square of dough over the top. You drop the vareniki into briskly boiling water and cook like noodles, until the pastry is cooked through and they rise to the top of the water. Remove them immediately from the water, drain, and serve them hot with sour cream and a sprinkling of sugar.

Bob and I liked vareniki, but like most young people, we were partial to chocolate confections. One of our favorite desserts was a very simple one, made of eggs and melted chocolate and called negritas.

NEGRITAS

Melt 3 ounces of bitter-sweet chocolate over hot water. Remove from fire, but leave over hot water while you stir in 3 well-beaten egg yolks, and a few grains of salt. Remove from hot water and flavor with vanilla or brandy. Beat the whites of the 3 eggs stiff and carefully fold them in before the chocolate mixture hardens. Pour immediately into glasses and chill for at least six hours before serving. Top each dish with a small mound of whipped cream and some finely chopped pistachio nuts or toasted almonds.

Another dessert that we enjoyed and which Katish was always happy to make for us, since the ingredients were sure to be on hand, was her burnt sugar pudding.

BURNT SUGAR PUDDING

In a heavy pan, over a low fire, caramelize 1 cup of granulated sugar. Add 1½ cups of boiling water and let the mixture simmer until it forms a smooth syrup. In the meantime, cube 3 slices of stale bread and place the cubes in a deep baking dish, first buttering the bottom, but not the sides, of the dish. Then scald 2½ cups of milk. Beat 3 whole eggs until frothy, and add ½ teaspoon salt and 1 teaspoon of vanilla. Pour the hot milk over the eggs and mix well. Pour the caramel syrup into the baking dish, over the bread cubes. Then put in the unsweetened custard. Sprinkle the top lightly with nutmeg. Put the pudding into a pan of water and bake in a moderate oven. Turn up the fire at the last and brown the top of the pudding well. The bread cubes will come to the top of the custard and form a delicious crust, and most of the syrup will remain in the bottom of the dish to be spooned up as a sauce for the pudding.

There wasn't anything very wonderful about our enthusiasm for Katish's desserts. But Mother had been pleased to see that we could get excited about vegetables, too, as Katish prepared them.

Katish carefully tended an herb garden near the kitchen door, where she could keep an eye on it. For Julio was strictly forbidden to trespass there. Katish warned him that she would certainly turn the hose on him if she ever found him intruding on her precious plot. Lovingly she cared for her "farm," as she called it, for some regular contact with the earth seemed to be a necessity for her. Dill and chives and parsley and tiny green onions grew like magic under her hand. And sweet basil, and other more mysterious herbs flourished there, too.

Dill does wonderful things for many vegetables. Thinly sliced, chilled tomatoes sprinkled with finely chopped dill and served with a sharp French dressing, lightly flavored with garlic, are a perfect salad.

String beans are delicious if they are cooked whole, tied in bundles to keep them tidy so that they can be stacked on a hot platter, then a sour cream and dill sauce poured over the top.

SOUR CREAM SAUCE

Make a medium white sauce, substituting 1 cup of sour cream for one of milk in a standard 2 cup recipe. Season well with salt and pepper, a tiny pinch of mustard, and add an herb which complements the flavor of the vegetable to be served with the sauce.

New potatoes to be eaten with tender pink slices of baked ham are extremely good in the sour cream sauce with a sprinkling of the dill. For tiny boiled beets, add chopped chives to the sauce. A head of boiled, well-drained cauliflower benefits wonderfully if it is covered with sour cream sauce, sprinkled lightly with grated cheese and parsley, then set under the broiler flame to bubble and brown.

For artichokes Katish served a butter and crumb sauce. Into each portion of melted butter, you simply stir enough very fine, lightly browned bread crumbs to make a sauce that will adhere to the hot artichoke leaves as they are dipped. Season the sauce well with salt and freshly ground black pepper.

Katish's fresh green asparagus and egg sauce was something to make anyone stand up and cheer. We often had it for a one-dish luncheon.

KATISH'S ASPARAGUS WITH EGG SAUCE

For each serving of fat green asparagus spears melt 3 tablespoons of butter. Have ready 1 hot hard-boiled egg for each person. Chop the eggs and stir them into the melted butter, season with a tiny pinch of mustard, salt, and fresh black pepper, quite coarsely ground. To make a more substantial dish, prepare a slice of toast for each serving; cover the toast with a thin, hot slice of ham, arrange the asparagus over the ham, and pour the hot egg sauce over all.

When Mr. Krasnoperov rose from the table after enjoying one of Katish's fine dinners, he always kissed Mother's hand, and Katish's too, if she happened to be in the room. He did it so easily

and matter-of-factly that we thought little of it. When he greeted Mother, and when he said goodbye, Mr. Krasnoperov repeated the hand-kissing. Some of the other Russian men among our acquaintances, particularly the older ones, did the same. But no one ever kissed Aunt Martha's hand. And Mother guessed that her sister-in-law felt a little resentful of this neglect. Aunt Martha never did a thing to mar the perfect white softness of her rather pretty hands, while Mother and Katish were forever digging around those extravagant dozens of rose bushes, and they didn't always remember to wear gardening gloves.

Finally Mother asked Katish about the etiquette of hand-kissing. The answer left her in a tight place, for she couldn't explain it to Aunt Martha without emphasizing the fact that Aunt Martha was an old maid. It is the Russian custom, Mother learned, to kiss only the hands of married ladies. They do this as frequently and as matter-of-factly as an American shakes hands. But a Russian gentleman never kisses the hand of an unmarried lady—not publicly and matter-of-factly, at any rate. Mother decided that it would be kinder to let Aunt Martha go on being puzzled about it and zealously applying hand lotion. It was one of those situations, Mother sighed, that just might solve itself. And soon it did.

Katish's Herb Garden

CHAPTER ELEVEN

Katish was peering anxiously from the doorway as Mother and I came up the garden path after a shopping trip one bright fall afternoon.

"Miss Martha is telephoning while you are away," she called urgently as Mother dawdled along, stopping to inspect the bronze chrysanthemums which were just coming into bloom.

"Did she leave any message?" Mother inquired, still bending over her flowers.

"Oh *da—da, da, da!* Yes. Important message! Mr. Krasnoperov has telephone to Miss Martha to say that he is ruined. He is killing himself on nice green brocade sofa in his office!"

"Good heavens!" Mother straightened up and gave Katish all her attention. "Has someone done something about it?" she asked, horrified but practical.

"I am making for Mr. Krasnoperov favorite dinner," Katish told her.

"What! How can the poor man possibly want any dinner if he's killed himself, Katish? You'd better go and lie down. Sis, call a taxi. I must get out there as fast as I can."

"No, I not lie down," Katish insisted. "Mr. Krasnoperov is promising to wait until Miss Martha comes. So I think is best to prepare good dinner. Miss Martha will not let poor fellow harm self, but he will still be ruined man. And ruined man needs good dinner."

On the whole, Mother thought, Katish might be right. Her confidence in Aunt Martha in time of emergency was certainly not misplaced. As for a ruined man's wanting a good dinner, that would depend on the man. It was as well to be prepared and it gave Mother and Katish something to do while they waited for the arrival of the unhappy man and his rescuer.

At last we heard the sound of a car in the drive and dashed to the window. A jaunty red roadster, top down, swerved alarmingly at our steps and stopped with a jolt, just as one tire grazed the masonry. In the roadster sat Aunt Martha and Mr. Krasnoperov. For a moment they just sat there, saying nothing, beaming fondly at each other. I nearly fell through the window at the sight of dignified Aunt Martha riding in such a rakish vehicle and looking pleased as Punch about it! Mother couldn't stand the suspense; she tapped on the window glass. The two in the roadster started rather guiltily, then looked up and waved at us. We met them at the door.

"Mr. Krasnoperov—I'm so glad to see that you're all right!" Mother exclaimed. "And you've got a lovely new car! You haven't run over someone, have you?" she finished, her bright tones faltering as she remembered the uncertain course of the red roadster up our drive, and that Mr. Krasnoperov was supposed to be a ruined man.

"No. I not kill anyone—not even poor useless self. You see!" Mr. Krasnoperov turned slowly around, exhibiting himself, solidly intact. "Is Martha, the dar-rrling Martha, who have save everything. She tell. But I am tell first of all—Martha she marry me and so I am forever save!"

"You are married!" Mother exclaimed, sitting down suddenly.

"No! Let's all sit down," Aunt Martha suggested sensibly.

"It's just Nicolai's English. We're not married yet," she explained. "But we are going to be." She blushed and almost dimpled. "We got engaged this afternoon when Nicolai promised not to kill himself."

Mother and Katish nobly swallowed their curiosity while they offered congratulations and best wishes.

"But what happened, Aunt Martha?" I urged. "I thought Mr. Krasnoperov was going to kill himself because he was ruined. And now you calmly say you're only going to get married!" Aunt Martha's engagement, though we had all so long looked forward to it, came as a bit of a letdown after the promise of greater excitement. Remembering that first, long ago fiancé of Aunt Martha's who was supposed to have drowned the week before the wedding was to have taken place, I'd begun to think we had a *femme fatale* in the family!

"Well, it was Nicolai's English that started all the trouble in the first place," my aunt told us. "He had a new and very important client—a retired movie actor of great wealth. Nicolai was doing his entire house over for him. There was some delay about the new tiles for one of the bathrooms and the actor telephoned two or three times a day about it. Nicolai was doing his best to hurry the work, I'm sure, and put the client off as best he could. But today the man called and was quite nasty. Nicolai got confused and said, rather angrily, I'm afraid, 'I will most certainly send undertaker for you tomorrow.'

"What Nicolai meant was, of course, that he'd send the contractor with the tile tomorrow."

"Yes. That what I mean," Mr. Krasnoperov interrupted. "I think undertaker is same as contractor. Is not true that contractor undertakes to do work? Martha explains me this but I still think most confusing that contractor undertakes but is not undertaker."

Aunt Martha took the narrative firmly into her own hands. "The client is a stupid sort of creature and he thought Nicolai was threatening him. I suppose his conscience told him he deserved some punishment for bothering poor Nicolai so much about the tile. He still had three bathrooms in perfectly good order. But to make a long story short, he declared that he was going to call the police and canceled the decorating order. Nicolai had put a lot of money into things for the house and he'd just bought his car, so he thought he was ruined."

"Oh yes, I am ruined, Dushinka, until you come and straighten everything out." Mr. Krasnoperov and our aunt exchanged mutually adoring glances.

"Well, I did manage to straighten it all out. Nicolai is still alive and the client is pacified," she admitted with self-congratulatory frankness.

We all sighed with relief. No one had thought of laughing while the recital was going on. It was Mr. Krasnoperov who suddenly saw the humor of his recent distressing situation. He began to smile and then to chuckle. At last he roared. We all laughed with him until we were weak.

Mother brought out the best brandy and the grown-ups drank to the coming wedding. Bob came in and he and I split a Coke in celebration.

The Coke must have gone to Bob's head. He knew how much Aunt Martha hated us to call Nicolai Krasnoperov by the English equivalent of his amusing name—Mr. Redfeather. But Bob cast caution to the winds. "Oooo-wah! Hurrah for Big Chief Redfeather!" he sang out suddenly and went hopping around the room in a wild impromptu Indian dance. In a flash Mr. Redfeather was on his feet behind Bob, circling and shouting. I joined the line-up. Around and around we went, mad with joy and excitement, doing something that must have looked like a cross between an Indian tribal dance and a prophetic forecast of the conga line. It wasn't surprising to us to have Mr. Redfeather join in an Indian dance. He'd told us many times of his early love for the Russian translations of Fenimore Cooper. He swore that he could quote pages and pages, word for word, he remembered the tales so well. It was impossible to tell whether the boast was true or not after Cooper's words had run the hazard of Mr. Redfeather's remarkable English.

When we calmed down enough to think of seeing how Aunt Martha was taking it, she was actually smiling indulgently. After all, she'd had quite a day! There was nothing in the world she loved better than straightening out other people's muddles—unless it was getting herself engaged!

"I hope you and Nicolai will take a house near us," Mother said to Aunt Martha at dinner.

"Well—we haven't had time to think where we'll live yet," Aunt Martha said. "The baron and I will have to talk that over later."

The Baron and Baroness Nicolai A. Krasnoperov!

"The baron?" Mother was puzzled.

"Oh, I haven't told you! So much has happened today!"

"Yes." Mr. Redfeather broke into the conversation without realizing, apparently, that Mother *still* hadn't been told. "My Martha, she has save me from so much today. I am afraid of nothing any-more. You remember, Mrs. Thurston—Mary, I have tell you long time ago, at Easter, I have two great wishes? And you advise me to make wish I have had longest."

"Yes. I thought I knew your more recent wish," Mother smiled.

"Yes, Mary. You are wise woman. I wish Martha to marry me. But I am not realize then, that if she marry me, I need no other wish. Martha take care everything."

"And what was that other wish? Does it have something to do with a baron?" Mother probed.

"Yes. It certainly does. Nicolai is the baron," Aunt Martha explained with obvious satisfaction. "You remember, Mary, how upset he was when I asked him once if he hadn't some title—that of baron, perhaps—which he would be entitled to use in his business? Nicolai was upset because he didn't want anyone to guess that he was a baron. It seems that he had some ancestor with his exact name who was very cruel and made implacable enemies. Nicolai was afraid that he might be confused with this man and sought out for punishment by some revolutionary character."

"So I am making wish this not happen to me," Nicolai told us all gravely.

"And you were able to fix this, Martha?" Mother asked, smiling. "I wonder how."

"I just told Nicolai that it was all nonsense!" Aunt Martha said firmly. "How could anyone possibly confuse Nicolai with anyone who was cruel and ruthless? And anyway, this is America. Everyone is safe here."

"I safe now," Nicolai repeated as he gazed with flattering confi-dence at his beloved.

I thought it was wonderful that my aunt Martha was going to be a baroness. It seemed to make her feel kinder toward all the world, too—or so we thought, for she only smiled indulgently at antics that had formerly won her stern disapproval. And she continued to ride with pleasure in Mr. Redfeather's undignified red roadster. She even said she thought she'd have to get her long hair cut, so that the wind wouldn't play such irreparable havoc with her coiffure when they went riding with the top down! But Aunt Martha could be relied upon to have some surprise in store for us.

"When you're the Baroness Redfeather—" I began one day.

"But I'm not going to be a baroness," Aunt Martha interrupted me.

"Oh, Martha, what do you mean?" Mother asked in dismay.

Aunt Martha was pleased with the interest that her simple statement had created. She laughed at my big-eyed surprise and Mother's worried look. "Nicolai and I have talked it over," she explained, satisfaction and regret mingled in her voice, "and we both feel that it is much more important for him to be a citizen of this country than to retain his title. We went last week to apply for his first papers. But, of course," she went on, "a few people do know about the title now, and though we shall never be able to use it officially, and as you know, Mary, I'm the last person in the world to put on airs, I suppose we can't stop people from thinking of us as the baron and baroness."

Mother smiled. "I am so happy for you," she told her sister-in-law.

"And by the way, Mary," Aunt Martha said in the kind, firm voice she always used when she meant to put something over, all for your own good, of course, "Nicolai and I will take Katish off your hands after we're married next month."

Mother was speechless for a moment. But, "Take Katish!" she finally gasped. "But we couldn't possibly get along without Katish. Oh, no! Martha," Mother said, and there was steel in her soft tones. "I couldn't give Katish up just when the children are growing up and going away. But I'll tell you what I'll do. I'll find a good Russian cook for you and Nicolai while you are on your honeymoon, if you like!"

SOME RECIPES FROM

KATISH'S OWN NOTEBOOK

CHICKEN A LA KIEV

Prepare 4 chicken breasts of small fryer size by cutting away all the bone except a short length of the top of the wing. Make tiny lengthwise slits in the flesh and fold it out as flat as possible. Be careful not to tear or break the meat. Pound gently with a wooden meat mallet, and cut any tendons in one or two places. Divide 6 tablespoons chilled sweet butter into 4 even portions of 1½ tablespoons each, mold the butter into round bars, and place one at the end of each piece of chicken breast. Sprinkle with 1 scant teaspoon salt. Now roll the chicken around the butter firmly and compactly. The piece of wing bone should protrude at one end, giving the bundle somewhat the appearance of a chicken leg. Tie each bundle together with a fine string. Dip the bundles in cold milk, drain well, and roll in flour. Add 1 scant teaspoon salt to 2 well-beaten eggs. Dip the chicken bundles in the eggs and roll them in fine bread crumbs. Repeat the egg and crumb treatment once more, making sure that the bundles are completely coated. Fry immediately in deep hot fat (370°) for five to ten minutes, or until the chicken is well browned on all sides.

BRANDIED PEACHES

Pare as many clingstone peaches as desired and place them in quart mason jars. Fill up all the empty spaces and cover the peaches with sugar. Put the jar lids on, but do not screw them down tightly, and omit rubbers. Inspect the peaches every day and continue to add more sugar to cover the peaches until the juice is drawn from them and the sugar is dissolved. When all the sugar has been dissolved and the peaches are covered with juice, insert the jar rubbers and tighten the caps. Wrap each jar in a good thickness of newspaper and store in a dark, dry place. In three months' time you will have delicious brandied peaches to serve over ice cream or pudding, and a liqueur that may be drunk or used in sauces.

CHICKEN CUTLETS POJARSKI

Combine 2 cups finely ground raw white chicken meat, ½ cup bread crumbs, soaked in cold milk and squeezed dry, and ½ cup softened butter. Add enough sweet cream, a little at a time, until the mixture can be molded readily. Add salt and pepper to taste, and just a suspicion of nutmeg. Form the mixture into small cakes, or mold in the form of chicken breasts, if desired. Dust well with flour and cook in clarified butter ½ inch deep in a heavy pan, over a moderate fire, until the cutlets are well browned on all sides. Serve with a mushroom sauce, or prepare a gravy with a few tablespoons of the drippings remaining in the pan, flour, seasonings, and sour cream.

KATISH'S DINNER BISCUITS

Sift together 1 cup of white flour, 1 cup of whole wheat flour (freshly ground if possible), ½ teaspoon of soda and 1½ teaspoons of salt. Work in 4½ tablespoons of butter, leaving the mixture in coarse lumps. Stir in just enough thick sour cream, about ¾ of a cup, to form a workable dough. Roll out ¼ inch thick. Fold the dough from all sides to form a square of about 4 or 5 inches. Roll out again, about ½ inch thick. Cut in small rounds, brush the tops with melted butter, and bake in a 450° oven twelve to fifteen minutes.

These biscuits will be thinner, crisper, richer, and saltier than the usual fluffy type served for breakfast. Excellent with salad, too, or with cheese. Split and buttered, they make an unusually good base for caviar and other, less exalted, appetizers as well.

COMPANY ROLLS

Scald 1 cup of milk and pour it over 1½ tablespoons of sugar, 1 teaspoon of salt, and ¼ cup of butter in a deep bowl. Cool the mixture to lukewarm, then add 1 cake of fresh yeast, crumbled. Beat in enough flour to make a thin batter and continue beating until smooth as satin. Fold in 1 egg white, stiffly beaten. Add more flour (making about 3½ cups in all) gradually to make a soft dough. Turn out on a floured board and knead the dough until it is smooth and elastic, adding more flour if necessary. Return the dough to the bowl, cover and let rise in a warm place until it is double in bulk.

Turn the dough out again and form into small balls. Place the balls on a buttered baking pan, lightly touching, but not crowding. Cover and let rise again for forty to sixty minutes. Bake in a hot oven (400°–425°) for about twenty minutes.

CASSEROLE OF SWEETBREADS

Parboil a pair of sweetbreads, then allow them to cool in cold water before removing the membranes. Dust them with flour and brown them quickly in a little butter on top of the fire in a small earthen casserole. Put the sweetbreads aside and brown ¼ pound of sliced fresh mushrooms, using more butter if necessary. Remove the mushrooms and brown 2 small carrots, 1 small onion, and 1 stalk of celery, all very finely chopped. Return the sweetbreads and mush-rooms to the casserole, add salt and pepper to taste, and pour in ½ cup of dry white wine and ½ cup of chicken stock. Cover tightly and place in a moderate oven (325°–350°) for twenty-five to thirty minutes. Remove the sweetbreads to a hot platter and thicken the gravy in the casserole with 1 scant teaspoon of flour. Pour the sauce over the sweetbreads and serve.

SHERRIED TONGUE

Simmer a smoked beef tongue in water containing a few pepper-corns, a bay leaf and a slice of onion. When tender, allow the tongue to cool in the broth. When cool enough to handle, remove the tongue and skin it carefully. Stick it with whole cloves and rub it with a small amount of Russian type mustard. Then spread with ½ cup of brown sugar to which 1 teaspoon of flour has been added. Put ½ cup of water into a small saucepan, add 3 tablespoons of tart currant jelly, and stir the mixture until smooth, over a low fire. Remove from the fire and add ½ cup of dry sherry. Pour the sauce over the tongue and place it in a moderate oven (350°) for thirty minutes, basting frequently.

BUFFET POTATOES

Boil 4 medium-sized potatoes in their jackets until tender but not soft. When cool enough to handle, slip off the skins and cut into ½-inch dice. Grate ½ cup of Gruyère cheese. Place a layer of potatoes in a buttered casserole; sprinkle lightly with flour, salt, and freshly ground pepper, then with grated cheese and a sprin-kling of finely chopped chives. Repeat the layers until all the potatoes are used, using 2 scant tablespoons of flour and 1 tea-spoon of chives in all. Pour 1 cup of rich milk over the mixture and dot the top with 2 tablespoons of butter. Set the casserole in a moderate oven (375°) for about forty minutes, until delicately browned.

These potatoes make a delicious hot dish for a buffet supper of hot or cold baked ham and green salad. They are too good and too subtle in flavor to be served "just as a change" with a rich meat course, says Katish.

CRAB OR LOBSTER SUPPER SANDWICHES

Sauté lightly 6 fresh mushroom caps, sliced, in 2 tablespoons of butter. Remove the mushrooms and stir 1½ tablespoons of flour into the remaining butter; stir gradually ¾ cup of light cream into this mixture to form a smooth sauce, and cook until thick, stirring constantly. Add 1½ cups of flaked crab or lobster meat, preferably fresh, the sautéed mushrooms, ½ teaspoon of onion juice, and salt and pepper to taste. Cook the mixture over a low fire for two or three minutes.

Blend 2 teaspoons of anchovy paste with enough butter to spread 4 English muffins fairly generously. Split the muffins, spread, and place them under the broiler for a minute, just until the butter bubbles. Cover each half muffin with some of the crab or lobster mixture, sprinkle with cheese (½ cup grated Gruyère or Parmesan in all), and replace them under the broiler until the cheese melts and browns delicately. It is preferable to prepare these on a fireproof platter that can be taken directly to the table.

GARDEN SALAD

Slice, but do not peel, 2 cucumbers. Slice 1 small sweet onion; trim and slice 1 bunch of crisp radishes. Spread these vegetables out on china plates, keeping the radishes separate, and sprinkle them all with 1 teaspoon of salt. This will make them "cry." Let them stand for thirty minutes in a cold place. Pour off the accumulated juice and dry the vegetables with a cloth. Combine them in a bowl. Beat 2 tablespoons tarragon vinegar and a little salt and ¼ teaspoon of freshly ground pepper into 2 cups of thick sour cream and pour this mixture over the vegetables. Toss lightly and serve very cold on crisp lettuce.

PLUM TOMATO CHUTNEY

Chop 3 pounds of large plums coarsely. Cut the tops from 1½ pounds of firm red tomatoes, press out and discard the seeds, then chop them coarsely. Grind finely 3 medium-sized onions, 1 clove of garlic, and 2 sweet red peppers. Place the mixture in a saucepan with 1½ cups each of brown sugar and white sugar, ½ cup of cider vinegar, 1 teaspoon of allspice, 6 whole cloves, 1 tablespoon of dry mustard, and 2 teaspoons of salt. Cook over a low fire and simmer gently, stirring frequently, for about forty minutes, or until it has thickened. Add 4 tablespoons of finely chopped ginger and cook for five minutes longer. Pour the mixture into sterilized jars and seal. Allow them to stand several days before using.

TARTAR PIROGUE
(a crisp honey cake)

Beat 2 whole eggs and 2 egg yolks together. Add 4 tablespoons of cream, then 2 tablespoons of sugar and 1 teaspoon of salt, and lastly 1 tablespoon of whisky. Beat the mixture well, then add enough flour to form a soft dough. Turn the dough out on a floured board and knead it for a few minutes. Roll out ¼ inch thick and cut in long, narrow strips. Cut across the strips to form tiny pieces the size of peas. Dust the "peas" with flour to prevent them from sticking together. Melt 2 pounds of vegetable shortening in a deep kettle; meanwhile remove all excess flour from the dough pellets by shaking them, a few at a time, in a sieve, then dusting in a towel. When the shortening is ready, drop in the pellets, a handful at a time. Fry until golden brown and drain on absorbent paper.

When all are fried and drained, place the pellets in a large bowl and stir in 2 cups of walnuts, coarsely broken, not chopped. Boil 1 cup of honey and 1 cup of sugar together over a low fire for five minutes. While the mixture still bubbles, pour it over the bits of fried dough and nut meats. Stir gently and thoroughly. Wet your hands and press the mixture into a well-buttered form. Let stand for at least three hours, then turn out by standing the form in hot water for a few minutes. Cut in thin slices with a sharp knife.

MARZIPAN TARTS

Prepare flaky tart shells. When cool, press into the bottom of each shell a ½-inch layer of plain marzipan. (Marzipan is available by the pound in small candy shops run by Austrian or Russian proprietors in most cities.) Fill the shells with a rich chocolate custard like that used in chocolate meringue pie. Top with whipped cream, very lightly sweetened and flavored with just a drop of almond extract.

APRICOT MERINGUE TARTS

Prepare 6 tart shells of flaky pastry. Cool them thoroughly and fill them with the following custard:

Beat 2 egg yolks and set aside. Mix and sift ¼ cup of sugar, 1 tablespoon of cornstarch, and a pinch of salt. Pour 1 cup of scalded milk over the sifted ingredients, stirring vigilantly. Stir the mixture over hot water until it has thickened. Pour half the hot custard mixture over the beaten egg yolks, stirring briskly, then stir this into the custard remaining in the pan. Cook for one minute longer, still stirring. Cool and flavor with vanilla. Fill the shells with the mixture and cover with apricot meringue made as follows:

Mash ½ cup of cooked dried apricots, which have been thoroughly drained, and put them through a sieve. Stir in 3 tablespoons of sugar. Beat 2 egg whites until stiff; fold in the apricots and beat until the mixture holds its shape. Cover the tarts with the meringue and brown them slightly in a moderate oven.

BANANA RUM CUSTARD

Scald 2 cups of rich milk; beat 2 egg yolks and add ¼ cup of sugar and a pinch of salt. Pour the hot milk over the egg mixture and blend well. Stir over hot water until the custard coats the spoon.

Meanwhile, soak 1½ tablespoons of gelatin in ¼ cup of cold water and add it to the hot custard mixture. Stir in 1½ cups of mashed bananas and 3 tablespoons of rum. Cool, and when the custard is just beginning to set, fold in 2 egg whites, stiffly beaten. Pour the mixture into a ring mold which has been rinsed in cold water and keep in the refrigerator until serving time. Fill the center of the mold with whipped cream, flavored with more of the rum if desired, and sprinkle generously with chopped pistachio nuts.

KASHA ROLL-UPS

Cook 1 cup of kasha (whole grain buckwheat groats) in 2 cups of boiling salted water over a low flame for fifteen minutes, adding a little more water if necessary. Let it cool, and stir in ½ cup of finely chopped, lightly browned onion and salt and pepper to taste. Cut thin beefsteak into individual portions for four, and rub with flour, salt, and pepper. Put some of the kasha on each piece of meat, roll it up, and skewer or tie securely. Brown the little beef rolls in hot fat and transfer them to a casserole with a tightly fitting cover. With the drippings remaining in the pan make enough brown gravy to cover the rolls. Stir in 1 cup of sour cream and 1 cup of sliced sautéed mushrooms and season well. Pour the gravy over the beef and kasha rolls and cook covered, in a moderate oven (350° to 375°) until the beef is tender.

KASHA AND MUSHROOMS

Cook 1½ cups of kasha in a little less than 3 cups of boiling, salted water for 10 minutes over a direct flame. Then set the pan over boiling water and steam for thirty minutes. Sauté ½ pound of sliced mushrooms in butter. Cut 1 large onion into thin rings, soak for a few minutes in cold milk, then dry the onion rings, toss them in seasoned flour, and brown them in hot fat. Put the hot kasha on a warm platter and arrange the onion rings around the edge. Pile the mushroom slices over the top and serve with a dish of sour cream.

DRAGOMIROVSKY FARSHMAK

Mix together in a buttered casserole 1 cup of diced, cooked smoked tongue, 1 cup each of diced, cooked ham and cooked cold chicken, 2 cups of diced, boiled potatoes, ½ cup of sautéed mushrooms, ¼ cup of browned onion or a little onion juice, 1 cup of sour cream, 1 tablespoon of tomato paste, and salt and pepper to taste. Toss all the ingredients until they are well blended and sprinkle the top with grated cheese. Cook in a hot oven (450°) until the mixture is heated through and brown on top.

INDEX

ABOUT THE AUTHOR

WANDA L. FROLOV wrote for *Gourmet* magazine for many years. Her stories of Katish first appeared there and were later gathered into a book in 1947.

A NOTE ON THE TYPE

The principal text of this Modern Library edition
was set in a digitized version of Janson,
a typeface that dates from about 1690 and was cut by Nicholas Kis,
a Hungarian working in Amsterdam. The original matrices have
survived and are held by the Stempel foundry in Germany.
Hermann Zapf redesigned some of the weights and sizes for Stempel,
basing his revisions on the original design.